THE BOHEMIAN

CARL MELANSON

THE BOHEMIAN

First Edition

Copyright © Carl Melanson 2021

Published by Amazon

CHAPTER ONE

I am a crow in the heavens…

The story of my life is an incredible one, mostly because of the things that didn't happen. My real life began the day I awoke in Hotel Chelsea and found a book on my escritoire tilted: "Amlethus." I say real because in a lot of ways I had never truly been awake. My troubles before that fateful day had been overwhelming---the worst of them being my mother's suicide. My life was like "The Bohemian Rhapsody," but in reverse… which I know is diabolical.

I remember when I was about four-years-old, my mother was hanging the laundry on the clothesline, and I asked her why the grass kept growing. She shrugged and said: "It just does, Solomon. Why do you need to know everything?" I think that's my first memory. I'm not sure, though---I have a terrible memory. When I think back, my mind starts wheeling around, like a broken time machine in Zanzibar.

I remember I used to dream about leaving San Francisco and becoming somebody else altogether. Miserable people are eccentric: emotional hoarders; flightless birds of a spiritual insolvency; patrons of a false expediency---to depart and sally forth like acumen in a vortex.

To me, a distorted, woolly reality seemed better than the one at hand, and so I walked among ignoble zealots and kept mostly to myself---especially at school. I was and always have been a loner: a counter-culture Libertarian, with a laisser-faire attitude.

And so drugs became a sort of osmosis for my mind… but I was also a schizoid… which is like a dysphasia for the soul, an inability to sparse the intellect beyond the interims of infinity.

The reason I would eventually lose my mind was simple: my thought-process had become too complicated and hyperactive. I became schizophrenic, almost overnight… like some kind of holistic Gemini, which controls my other hemisphere: a subconscious daemon in the shunts of my persona... haunted by the red herring of duplicity---such is the veneer of my illness: schizophrenia.

As an artist, I have bouts and stints of depression, almost on the daily basis: my thoughts tend to stray like vagrants on a carousel.

But don't jump ahead of me and think that I was just some kind of drug addict no-hoper in a dotard's ego trip. I simply didn't draw any attention to my suffering; it was like a steeplechase for my emotions---and I always lost.

***

After the divorce with Joseph, my mother and I moved to another city when I was twelve-years-old---Greenwich Village: to live in NY habitat, in a furnished apartment close to the bohemian antinomy of the town's subculture.

She had always dreamed of going to New York because she was an editor-in-chief... and New York was a Mecca for creativity in the arts and the humanities.

Meanwhile, my little brother Charlie stayed in San Francisco with Joseph, simply because he was his biological father.

I have to tell you, going from a place like San Francisco to a place like Greenwich Village was frightening for a twelve-year-old boy from such a Podunk little town---comparatively. I remember the first time I saw New York City, clouded in smog and traffic noise, the hubbub of vanities, Capitalist slogans hovering above protest crowds, gay parades, and all sorts of other things that seemed to siphon excitement into peoples' monochrome, prosaic lives.

I'd never seen anything like it...

Changing schools again was terrible, and so I avoided the other students as much as I could. I've always been poles apart--- that's why I like to read so much. Literature to me was a Leonard Cohen afterworld: an escape, in which I flew from life's dispersions, and I loved getting lost in it like a rueful saint, like Tolstoy, which is also why I was now growing my beard. I wanted to look and dress like an intellectual: erudite and bookish, like Samuel Beckett... my favourite dramaturge. I especially loved "Krapp's Last Tape," and I read it incessantly like a spool…

After I graduated from high school, I read all sorts of literature on my own time---not the books they would get you to read in class. For me, literature was like an ambo for the emeritus within us, struggling with the truth, merely to ascertain that it cannot be beaten down by the nilpotent and apical accruals of sanctity in the arts… like lightning in a spire, or a gargoyle made of glass.

My favourite book was "The Catcher in the Rye" by J.D. Salinger, because Holden Caulfield was a loner just like me. All the other students ever read were the books the teacher would give them to read in class---it was just for grades, and never for smarts. Those books were always about magical anecdotes, or pirates, and all sorts of other bullshit about the Artic tundra.

I hated books like that with all my revilement…

I disparaged it all as nonsense and nothing more…

That's why I wanted to become a poet, a writer---even as schizophrenia kicked in the door to my mind like a Nilotic train. I was now a Slavic in a room full of parables, that I could not spiel without contingencies to rise against my rue…

In that sense, I wanted to be like Arthur Rimbaud, a rebel poet who balks against tradition, to ascertain his prose simply to contemn it as dissent.

No one is born to be a genius… you have to surround yourself with knowledge---the pursuit of knowledge is the most noble pursuit of all.

Genius, the god within, comes from a repertoire of Gnosticism about your own craft, whatever it may be… like javelins thrown into the Sun: a pawl for the nuisance of your rhetoric---an aphelion around your juxtaposition against your own Apgar score.

***

Meanwhile, my mother had landed a better job. She was head nurse at the hospice now, so she could always tell when I was malingering and flaccid. "Nice try," she'd say and pull the covers off me. And I would try to put her on some more, whining about how much my stomach was in the Spunginghouse.

In the interim, my mother couldn't understand why I didn't want to go to school in the morning, because when I did I would get it really bad---especially in the gym class. They would always bully me and browbeat me in the locker-room, like stupid brutes, and I was left to abide as a colorless protégé of sorrow and suicidal despondency---it was an albatross that I could scarce obviate, nor preclude within myself. They would throw food at me and launch their shoes at me like it was a sport, a diversion of sorts---a Babylonian sideshow, wherein I was the outsider, the reprobate, the loser: a Theban scoundrel of thecae-like regression into the self: schizophrenia.

After a while, you suffer so much that it doesn't really affect you anymore… you become numb and lacklustre, and that was my goal after all---a simpatico for the ephemera of a ghost: enlightenment among my scruples.

It was an indictment for my soul, an arraignment for my mind, all against the nuances of the everlasting light of literature, "the eternal affirmation of the spirit of man," which is also my art to bauble the mock sceptre within… the ego.

If you're creative and unique, teachers just hate you for it---originality is prohibited in the schools of America. They just want to homogenize our brains with their regiments to get us ready for the New World Order like mindless slaves---just intelligent enough to function, like automatons…

I wanted to be an outsider artist, like Henry Darger… I also wanted to be a lifetime virgin, completely celibate, like Tesla and Newton: a monk in a refuge of helotism and symbiosis.

In that regard, I was like a nematode: I was protected by my own cuticle...

My mother would always call me a hermit, so I'd get smart with her and call her a "pusillanimous termagant" or something that she didn't quite understand. I'd read the dictionary a dozen times just because I was bored, and I wanted to learn as many words as possible, like James Joyce…

'The more you expand your vocabulary, the more you expand your mind' …

To me, that's just the work of a writer these days---but internally my thoughts tend to waft like diodes because of my illness…

That's why I like to write down my own agitprops for Metamodernism. I have a hyperactive brain---full of dopamine and epinephrine, like acetones in the atom, of which I am made to dream upon infinity... the infinity of the human mind, which I must reclaim as my own arbiter:

Metamodernist // Manifesto

Luke Turner

1.
We recognize oscillation to be the natural order of the world.
2.
We must liberate ourselves from the inertia resulting from a century of modernist ideological naivety and the cynical insincerity of its antonymous bastard child.
3.
Movement shall henceforth be enabled by way of an oscillation between positions, with diametrically opposed ideas operating like the pulsating polarities of a colossal electric machine, propelling the world into action.
4.
We acknowledge the limitations inherent to all movement and experience, and the futility of any attempt to transcend the boundaries set forth therein. The essential incompleteness of a system should necessitate an adherence, not in order to achieve a given end or be slaves to its course, but rather perchance to glimpse by proxy some hidden exteriority. Existence is enriched if we set about our task as if those limits might be exceeded, for such action unfolds the world.
5.

All things are caught within the irrevocable slide towards a state of maximum entropic dissemblance. Artistic creation is contingent upon the origination or revelation of difference therein. Affect at its zenith is the unmediated experience of difference *in itself*. It must be art's role to explore the promise of its own paradoxical ambition by coaxing excess towards presence.

6.

The present is a symptom of the twin birth of immediacy and obsolescence. Today, we are nostalgists as much as we are futurists. The new technology enables the simultaneous experience and enactment of events from a multiplicity of positions. Far from signaling its demise, these emergent networks facilitate the democratization of history, illuminating the forking paths along which its grand narratives may navigate the here and now.

7.

Just as science strives for poetic elegance, artists might assume a quest for truth. All information is grounds for knowledge, whether empirical or aphoristic, no matter its truth-value. We should embrace the scientific-poetic synthesis and informed naivety of a magical realism. Error breeds sense.

8.

We propose a pragmatic romanticism unhindered by ideological anchorage. Thus, *metamodernism* shall be defined as the mercurial condition between and beyond irony and sincerity, naivety and knowingness, relativism and truth, optimism and doubt, in pursuit of a plurality of disparate and elusive horizons. We must go forth and oscillate!

Luke Turner's syllabus proves that your ability to understand complicated things is what makes you intelligent, whether it's literature or science: with metaphors and figures of speech expounding what is also transparent within us, to what invokes the truth to be seen as such: ekistics for the soul---hamlets made of light, or staccatos between heaven and hell... for such is the fault in our stars.

And such is my purpose as a writer, and an Orwellian disciple:

write whatever the fuck you want---that's Metamodernism.

***

One of the philosophers I would learn about from my older brother in New York, Hobbes, used to sleep with a gun under his pillow. He was an anti-social just like me---a loner. It's like I said, I don't talk unless spoken to, but if the subject is interesting, worthy of note, I can talk for hours, especially when I'm high or drunk. I like intelligent conversations about politics, literature, philosophy, and art history.

Knowledge and understanding tend to reckon the oghams of the human mind like repartees left and right---the doors of a hostel on either side, to subsume our intelligence with rational and cogent arguments, and thus ignite our own argots like a siren song for the obtuse.

It's a labyrinth for those who yet do not understand the labyrinth. Thus endow your sorrow with wisdom as an armour, and you shall escape the defilades of helotism within your squire, which reverses the entropy of truth, like an Entebbe made of pantropic umbrages.

Indeed, antipathy to me breeds like colza in the solstice of imperfection, a rapacious little stint of cambia, ingrained in relativity.

If you stop sinning you will stop suffering, and if you stop suffering you will stop sinning.

Indeed, such a berceuse extinguishes the truth, like urchins that regret the cosmos to set alight their integrity---a cryogenic memory, or a vestibule in the psyche.

It's all stream-of-consciousness…

***

I remember, when I was fifteen-years-old, I tried to read a book by Howard Zinn, and I got so depressed and crestfallen that I couldn't even finish reading it…

I thought I knew everything I needed to know, and so school

was boring to me---a total waste of time... I wanted to become a writer, a Metamodernist writer---we must go forth and oscillate!

And so I was writing feverishly everyday---mostly poetry and prose. I was currently working on a novel called: "AMLETHUS."

Amlethus means Hamlet in Latin---Am-leth-us. Sometimes I'd get so obsessed with what I was writing that I would go on for ten hours, stopping only to grab a bite to eat across the street at a Delian café. Even as I ate my meal, I kept processing the possibilities of my linguistic style, my prosody, everything I could possibly think of as part of my Esperanto, my rhapsody. I was obsessed with language: how it worked, how it moved, how it sounded, how it did just about anything you want it to do. If you want to be the best, you have to learn from the best, and Shakespeare sets the criterion for the ortho-doxies of literature, like a nodule in the requiems of presage and augury.

So I started reading a bunch of crazy books, like "Nightwood," and "Ulysses." I especially read the controversial ones, the ones that had been burned at some point in history, like Wilde's "Salome," or "Portnoy's Complaint," by Philip Roth...

But I especially read existentialist kitsch, like Beckett, Gaddis, Joyce, and, of course, a gargantuan amount of Shakespeare. He was a biological freak with all the right fabrics to weave a plot into a dismaying caricature of human acclivity into the heaths of literature...

Nowadays, people listen to really stupid music, so I sought my pleasures elsewhere, whenever I went to HMV. I started listening to Elliott Smith and Bob Dylan. The first time I listened to "Blonde on Blonde," I couldn't get passed his voice, but then I listened to it while high, and it blew my fucking mind.

I especially liked "Stuck Inside of Mobile with the Memphis Blues Again." Also, I would often go to the bookstore and look for something good to read, like poetry anthologies, or books and novels by Nobel laureates.

But this one time, something happened that would change my life forever. It's one of those things that you don't even realize changed your life until it's over and done with. It's like they say: "If you don't appreciate your life now, you'll be wistful later."

***

Later that day, I was walking around and I heard some applause. Someone was doing a poetry reading on the other side of the Barnes and Nobles, near the coffee shop. So I decided to go and have a look for myself. I sat down among the crowd and started listening without my clique in mind. I later found out that it was Irving Layton, the famous Canadian poet from Montreal. He was really charismatic in that intellectual kind of way. Indeed, he was witty and intelligent, like a medieval scop---I think he was a Jew. Northrop Frye once said of him: "He has a poetic mind of genuine dignity and power…"

It's an agonal thing to ascertain another poet's genius without envy…

He soon began to read a poem called "Cain." It was about a father teaching his son to kill a frog. The imagery was so absurd I could barely hold back my chuckles, but it seemed like the others weren't getting it like I was. They were thinking about the negative aspects of the poem. Irving Layton even ended his poem with a line that said there was a joke that we didn't quite hear. I'll tell you all about it. The poem was about a father teaching his son how to kill a frog. But the frog gets away. And the father goes on imagining how absurd its life will become. The poem ends like this:

When the next morning I came the way
The frog was on his back, one delicate
Hand on his belly, and his white shirt front
Spotless. He looked as if he might have been
A comic; tapdancer apologizing
For a fall, or an emcee, his wide grin
Coaxing a laugh from us for an aside
Or perhaps a joke we didn't quite hear.

The rather short shaggy-dog story in the poem was that the

father never even realized how absurd it was to assert his existence by killing something as simple as a frog, which thereby steers his conscience to the precipice without falling. I don't know what was wrong with the rest of the crowd. They looked so serious and bleak-faced, like intellectuals in Pompeii. They weren't even there to listen, like they knew something that no one else could possibly know.

But there was this one girl who seemed like she'd actually gotten the joke, serious as it was. So after every poem I would just look at her to see her reaction but this one time she looked at me and caught me looking. I couldn't help but blush and look away. I looked at her again and she smiled. And this is how it all began---with a simple smile.

***

Ami Eston had long silky black hair and a rather contagious smile. She just seemed so pure to me at the time, even though I knew nothing about her. After the reading, I was standing outside, waiting for the bus. I heard Ami coming from behind me. She suddenly slipped on some ice and shrieked. As she lay on the ground, I crouched over and asked her if she was okay. For some reason, she started laughing wildly. Hearing her laughing at herself, I couldn't help but laugh as well.

She got up and said: "Don't look in this direction, you're gonna fall in love…"

I laughed, and we started talking at the bus stop…

"Do you live far?" she asked.

"Greenwich Village," I said.

"Oh God… that is far."

"Doesn't matter," I said. "I like to get lost and find myself again…" I paused. "What's your name?"

"Ami Eston… what's yours?" she asked.

"Solomon Roy," I said.

She smiled at me with her eyes.

I noticed she was holding a pocket sized Emily Dickinson poetry book I her hand---a 'Shambhala Pocket Classics.' I didn't want the conversation to run dry, so I asked her: "Do you browse through it much?"

"Emily Dickinson? All the time... What about you?" she asked.

"Every now and then..." I said. "I love poetry... My mother introduced me to Shakespeare when I was eleven... I've been hooked ever since."

"Yeah, well, my mother's an agnostic... a Communist..."

"That's very unsettling." I said and chuckled.

"Yeah, she's a hippie at heart. She even went to Woodstock in 1969... She keeps joking that it's why I'm a singer-songwriter at heart..."

"You're a singer-songwriter?" I asked.

"Yes... I am."

"So am I..." I said.

"No kidding..."

"Dead serious... and I'm actually pretty good at it. At least that's what people say..."

"Do you toke up sometimes?" she asked.

"Every now and then, but I don't go too crazy with it, though."

"Does your mother know?" she asked.

"Yeah... She doesn't really approve..."

"My mother's an artist," she said. "A painter..."

"A painter?" I asked.

"Yeah, and just about everything else you can think of..."

"She is exactly what I wanna be," I said.

"You're an artist? Do you paint?" she asked.

"I mostly write, but I've been painting a lot more lately. It's kind of an expensive habit..."

"Maybe you should come over sometime and show her your work." She looked away shyly.

"Yeah, I'd like that." I said. "Get some good constructive criticism from a real artist. Does she ever do exhibitions?"

"Yeah, she's got one right now at an Art Gallery in Greenwich Village."

"Are you going anywhere near Greenwich Village?"

"That is where I live..."

"Oh... maybe we should just wait for the next bus then."

When the bus arrived, we continued our conversation, tête-à-tête, like an Aesop Rock rap session about nothing in particular. This kind of thing had never happened to me before. It was only once I met Ami that I really opened up to the world. It felt good, to tell you the truth. She wasn't judging me like people usually did, she just took me as I was. For someone like me, this is like a spiritual revelation. It struck me more deeply than she could have ever known; like Fehling's solution on diabetics: I was immediately mesmerized.

"What are you thinking about?" I asked.

"I was just thinking about how Irving Layton's eyebrows keep trembling when he gets nervous. They always shake around when he's doing interviews and stuff. Don't get me wrong, I love Irving Layton. That's why I went to see him read, but it's just so peculiar. Why the eyebrows? I just found it cute in that old man kind of way." She paused for a moment... "It's nothing weird or anything... it's just... I don't know, they just have all this little antics and jokes and it just makes me laugh. Like my grandfather. When me and my sister would try to watch cartoons, he would just stand there until he found something to talk about even though none of us were listening. So he was just basically talking to himself. It was really funny. But, then again, those are the moments you end up remembering when someone you love passes on."

"When did he pass?" I asked.

"Couple of years ago..."

"Did you know him well?"

"Well enough," she replied. "I'd usually go there on the weekends, especially when I was eighteen or nineteen, because he'd read pretty much every book in the world and I always wanted to teach English."

"Seriously?" she asked.

"Yeah..." I said. "I looove literature. I'll read anything from Hemingway to Shakespeare... I like Hamlet a lot too. I've read it four times so far..."

"I read "The Old Man and the Sea" about three months ago."

"What did you think about it?" I asked.

"A lot of symbolism. Good symbolism. I actually thought about the old man when I first looked at Layton. It's kind of lame, but I imagined that he was the old man and I was the young boy helping him lug his things to his boat. I have a crazy mind like that… for some reason…" She paused. "So what's your favorite book of all time?"

"Ouff… the one that affected me the most is probably 'The Catcher in the Rye,' but the one I've read the most is 'Hamlet.' Five times and counting. But I mostly like stuff like 'Fear and Loathing in Las Vegas.'"

"That book's hilarious," she said. "I can't believe he actually went through that." She paused again. "What kind of music do you listen to?"

I said: "Mostly Bob Dylan, John Lennon, The Doors, Pink Floyd, Elliot Smith, Radiohead, Nirvana… stuff like that. Mostly music from the 60s. Do yourself a favour… listen to 'Blonde on Blonde' after you toke up. It'll blow your mind… but you have to smoke up first…"

"Wow… you actually have good taste." She noticed she was getting close to her house and so she pulled the string for the next bus stop. "This is the one." She looked at me. "Hey, I should give you my number…"

"Yeah, sure…" I said.

She reached into her purse and pulled out a pen and a piece of paper. After she wrote it down, she did something that surprised me, but it expressed her fearless charm perfectly as an osier. She leaned over and gave me a quick peck on the cheek. I knew at that very moment that I had met someone who would change my life forever. I just wondered if she felt the same way or if I was just a temporary plaything that she would discard as soon as she got bored. Either way, she was like amphetamine, and I was a falcon in a jess…

CHAPTER TWO

Meeting a girl in a bookstore had always been a dream of mine…

"It was amazing, mom. Her name's Ami Eston… she's the most beautiful girl I've ever met. She's smart, intellectual, graceful, sarcastic, kind of artsy but not like a posh at all… and she's a singer-songwriter just like me…"

I was in the kitchen with my mother. She was sitting solemnly at the table like a vanilla-skinned golliwog. "What's wrong?"

She forced a smile. "Solomon…" She sighed and then began to cry. "Oh God…"

"Mom… what happened? What's the matter?" I sat next to her and took her hand in mine.

"There's a reason I've been so worn out lately… I…" She stopped and looked at the ceiling as if to roll her eyes at herself. "I rehearsed how I would tell you but… I just can't get it out… I'm so sorry, Solomon…"

I stood up, getting frustrated, which stymied my sacrilegious pall---a spurious cog in my mother's defence mechanism, which was sheltered by her silence, like a monad in a gale.

"Just say it. For God's sake!"

She looked at me with such hopelessness… I couldn't stand it… it was like tears of brine in my eyes…

"Solomon… I've been diagnosed with schizophrenia. I've been going to see a psychiatrist lately and---he started me on Abilify… it's this new drug… it's really strong…"

"Why didn't you tell me about this, mom…?"

"It can't be helped, Solomon. It's just the way I am. I didn't choose this. It's just the biogenesis of my brain, I suppose…"

I sighed and sat down again. "So what happens now?"

"I have to start taking this medication every day…"

"Mom, you know I don't believe in that stupid bullshit. The side-effects'll just make it worse than it already is…"

"How can it make it worse? It's a pill, Solomon..."

"All psychiatrists do is help people to be helpless."

She sighed and said, "That's not true... I've had... a few episodes... hallucinations..."

"What d'you mean?"

"That's when I get so overwhelmed that I can't control my own thoughts and they just keep pecking at me..."

"Is it really the illness that does that?"

"Yes... I don't determine when it happens in my mind. It just hits me all of a sudden and I lose touch with reality..."

"How bad is it?" I asked.

"Schizophrenia...?" She laughed. "I'd rather get sodomized by a cactus..." I looked at her like I always do when she said something crazy, with repulse. And she just went on laughing in spite of herself. How a devout Christian could have such a dirty mind was beyond me. I accepted it over the years as an idiosyncrasy and nothing more...

In that sense, she was exactly like Esther Greenwood in Sylvia Plath's "The Bell Jar," which was also her favourite book...

***

There are some people in this world that, just by looking at them, you can tell are artists. Ami's mother was one of those people. The clothes she wore were colourful and cultural... She wore a strange shawl around her head, gigantic earrings and a fair amount of make-up. I could tell she was a heavy smoker by the wrinkles around her mouth and her slightly yellow teeth. It's not that she wasn't an attractive woman; she was quite stunning, especially when she was in her twenties. (I caught a glimpse of her wedding picture atop the piano and had to look away before she caught me gawking.) She had seen my reaction and she smiled slyly as she put out her frail hand to shake mine. She put it out in such a manner as if I was supposed to kiss it. Not my thing. I just shook it gently and let it go. She was definitely a Postmodernist bohemian, under the enchantment of Communism as the statehood of truth and freedom in her own mind, which I did not fully understand at the time.

"My name is Minerva, the goddess of wisdom." She laughed in spite of herself. She was quite ostentatious, like Katharine Hepburn on cocaine...

"I'm Solomon. Solomon Roy..."

"A prophet and a goddess," Ami said. "You two should get along..." she said and sneered at her mother.

"So Ami tells me you're an artist, a writer?" said Minerva. "What did you bring me...?" I had a painting in a garbage bag with me. I handed it to her and she brought it to the table. She pulled it out. The painting was about another painter that I had recently become obsessed with---Vincent van Gogh. In the bottom right corner was a replica of his "Self-Portrait." I had used that painting as a guide to paint Vincent in his room. Inside the frame of his bedroom window, I painted a small facsimile of "The Starry Night." All the shadows in the room turned into flames and van Gogh himself was holding a burning rose to represent his passion, his lust for life. Finally, his shadow prophesied the night he would eventually cut off his right ear and give it to a cocotte.

Minerva looked at it for a while. She looked at every detail. "Solomon... this is... amazing." I thought she was being a little bit obtuse, meaning she was probably lying. But, it turns out she really did love it.

"So... should I keep painting?" I asked.

She looked at me like I was joking. "Do you have more?"

"Not that much... I only have like twelve paintings done so far. It's kind of an expensive hobby."

"How long have you been painting?" she asked.

"Two years..."

"And you're a writer, too?" she asked.

"Yeah... but what I write is too eccentric to ever be published. I've been studying Metamodernism. It's really interesting. The manifesto online is a bit difficult but it's pure genius..."

"What do you mean?"

"It's just... I don't know, most publishers look for books that make them a lot of money. What I write is too ultramodern for them."

"They want a broad audience with narrow minds…" she said.

I laughed. "Yeah, I guess you could say that…"

Minerva looked just as clueless as me for a few moments and then remembered. "Oh yes... Ami and I were wondering if you'd like to come to the gallery to have a look at my work. Interested?" She paused and looked at me intently. "Well… now you don't have a choice. Let's go." She grabbed my arm and pulled me forward out of the apartment.

CHAPTER THREE

One day, after seeing a movie with Ami, I entered the apartment and I knew my mother was in distress. I could hear her moaning---carping her wits in the bathroom.

"Mom?" I walked over to the bathroom and knocked on the door. "Mom? Are you okay...?"

"Solomon...?"

I tried to open the door but it was locked. "Mom... unlock the door." My mind was pacing at a rate of knots... You have to understand that living with someone who has schizophrenia is like living with a drug addict. (I know, I'm a hypocrite---a salesman on a fen, a wooden nickel patriarch, all the way to death's dream kingdom!) It's unpredictable and frightening, like a ghost in a garret, in the eaves of perception that no one can bear without posterns of the self: schizophrenia.

Any day the individual can completely collapse into an unbearable sense of depression and societal angst, which cannot sheave the consequence of their choices, like a pictogram for mere reminiscence. And so she would always try to pointlessly transmogrify her pain from the mental to the visceral.

And when she did, it only made her feel even more worthless than her personal squire obliged---a pergola for her clueless arbitrage against her sainthood, like a piker in a tavern of fools. Her way of thinking would take the form of an abysmal coulee, a ravine of incertitude, and it was so terrifying to her that she never realized she could control it by turning the tide on her own presage, which prefigures the augur within like a bazaar of bad dreams and other such penny dreadfuls.

To her, the brain was an involuntary muscle, an uncultured prawn in dire need of self-discipline, but her lack of providence riddled her with fear and guilt. To this day, I can only vaguely summarize my deduction of her psychotic episodes.

I just couldn't see things from her perspective---the standpoint of her diagnosis.

As a writer, I should've been able to do that with the greatest of ease---but not with my mother. She had distorted her views of reality so much that I could only stand by her helplessly and ask her the same questions over and over again... She was not cloy at all about her illness, like a false acacia in the grounds of deceit---an ideogram for the matrix of an oarsman, with no vessel to prow into the quantum storms of self-hood: selfish DNA.

"Mom? Do you have your medicine with you? Do you need it...?"

"Umm..." Her voice was trembling. "No... I don't need it anymore. It's not good for me, Solomon. The doctor just wants me to... be a fucking guinea pig on Abilify. I can't eat... I can't sleep... I can't sit down for five seconds... I think I took too much... or not enough... I can't even tell anymore!"

She began to cry...

I'd heard this before. That's the thing about crazy people, they always have to convince themselves that they're not crazy, and that's what makes them so erratic, like gambits on a runaway convoy. My mother would create all sorts of specious logistics for herself, and she would feel so bad for creating them that she felt as if she had no other choice but to make it seem real. That way she didn't need to abide by the Thanatos rules of reality---she could create them for herself. If she decided that someone was bad or judgmental, she would pummel her mind with vain iterations to make her judgment justifiable as her own objectivism. Her suspicion of people was getting worse with every passing month---her distain against reality.

"Solomon... you don't understand..." She opened the door. "Let me show you something. This is how they do it." She was whispering. She grabbed my hand and pulled me to the living room. "Oh, Solomon... if only you could understand the way the world really works. They made the world into a giant marketplace." She was all over the place with her ideation. I was just concerned about giving her the medicine to get this over with. I always felt like crying when she was like this, but I stopped doing that because it just exacerbated her state of mind. "Solomon... It's just so the government can control it. They're even going to put microchips in people. It's the mark of the beast... a sku on the right hand or the forehead... look: 666."

"Mom, just---"

"And the All-seeing Eye... cameras everywhere. The Government is even watching us through our own television screens! Orwell was right, Solomon. Everything he said would happen is happening! It's all happening. And look..." She went to grab her Bible. She turned it to the book of revelation and showed me 13:16-18. "'And he causeth all, both great and small, rich and poor, free and bond, to receive a mark in their right hand or in their foreheads: and that no man might buy or sell, save he that hath the mark. Here is wisdom, let he that hath understanding count the number of the Beast: for it is the number of a man, and his number is 666.' It's the New World Order! I've been reading about it... Don't you see what's happening all over the news? Iraq! That's where Babylon was and in it's near the river Euphrates. It even says in the Bible that this is how the end of the world'll come about. Don't you see? It's the New World Order! A World Government, lead by the Antichrist! I'm not sick, Solomon. It's the world that's crazy, not me... it's bound to convince you that you're no better than one of the wicked. Don't let them microchip you... don't tell me they've got you convinced of this. I'm not crazy. Even astrologers are talking about it. Something's going to cause the world to literally go topsy-turvy. The north and south poles are going to be reverse and it's going to cause earth-quakes and volcanoes and all sorts of disasters. I'm just trying to tell you the truth, Solomon..."

I sighed. "I can't sleep here tonight, mom. I'm going back to Ami's apartment."

I just needed to get away and get high again...

CHAPTER FOUR

Indeed, I was in a cosmic maelstrom from which I could not oust myself...

The next morning, I woke up on Ami's floor, completely dishevelled from a night of tossing around mindlessly. She was still asleep and I knew she had a habit of sleeping in until 10AM, so I decided to get out of bed and go out for a cup of coffee. It was a cold morning, but when you've got something on your mind, the cold doesn't matter that much, especially in New York. The voice of desire just kind of drags you along from place to place, and I'm not one to silence it. I usually just go out on a whim, a caprice of notions and formations in the ego.

I've always been like that. I'll just be sitting there, doing nothing, and then something'll hit me, like a bushel of haggles, if that's even possible. Next thing I know, I'm buying another Beatles album---Sergeant Pepper. The greatest album of all time according to Rolling Stone magazine. Not sure if I agree with that. I've always liked "The Wall" by Pink Floyd: especially the movie.

I've watched it several times...

I got to Starbucks and ordered my usual medium double-double. The cashier knew me pretty well by now. I think her name was Devan. I'd gone to school with her but we had that peculiar kind of relationship where we'd just small-talk for a few minutes and then go about our business. She brought me my coffee and I thanked her. She saw that I'd brought a book with me and asked me what it was. I said, 'Crime and Punishment,' by Dostoevsky." It's about a genius who kills this old pawn-broker with an axe and his conscience gets the better of him." I just didn't like the translation. It was kind of... forced and unnatural. You could tell it wasn't the original language: unlike Edgar Allen Poe---one of my all-time favourites. I especially loved "The Telltale Heart," and "The Raven."

***

When I was alone, which was most of the time, I would always drink Absinthe in the hopes of seeing the green fairy in my most pensive daydreams, but it never happened because I think it wasn't real aniseed. Sometimes I would drink it just to give myself the boost of intellect I needed to write something meaningful. I was thinking of coming up with my own style of writing, my own -ism. As I sat there, I thought I could bring it up to Minerva to see what she thought, but I was always anxious when I talked to other bohemians about my work.

I have an inferiority complex, you see... that's why I'm always alone.

You tend to hang out with people who are at the same level as you are, whether socially or intellectually.

***

When I got back to Ami's apartment, she was awake, sitting on her computer chair in her underwear, watching a documentary about Bob Dylan titled "No Direction Home." I'd lent it to her the previous day...

She heard me and paused it...

"Where'd you go?" she asked.

"Get a cup of coffee at Starbucks across the street."

"You corporate schmuck. Why don't you go to the smaller coffee shops?"

"'Cause I like Starbucks... besides I'm a Capitalist." I said and sneered at her sarcastically.

"Don't tell my mother you went to Starbucks, she'll give you a whole speech about it. Trust me, you don't want to hear my mother's tirades about Capitalism. It's just her way of getting back to her Russian roots. Her grandfather was a Soviet... part of the nomen-klatura. He was a Communist writer back in the day..."

"But she doesn't even have an accent..."

"It only comes out when she's drunk or angry," she said.

I took off my coat and sat down next to her. "Well... I'm glad you told me, because I was going to tell her about this idea I had for a painting."

"What idea?" she asked.

"A painting with Tolstoy and Napoleon gambling together and drinking alcohol from each other's countries."

"Napoleon getting drunk with Tolstoy. You've read "War and Peace," right?"

"Yeah," I said. "That's how I got the idea. I was even going to get Napoleon's dog to hump Tolstoy's leg to make fun of his absurd stance on marriage."

"What stance?" she inquired.

"That sex is so vile and repugnant to God that even married people shouldn't fuck..."

Her mouth was agape with unbelief. "You really are a crazy artist." She shook her head. "It's so crazy, in fact, that I dare you to bring it up to my mom. Seriously..."

"You really want me to? 'Cause I'll do it."

"Maybe not... but be prepared for a long dialogue about the status quo. How informed are you about politics?"

"Well... sometimes I watch debates on CNN."

Now she was really laughing at me. "Wow... Okay, you know nothing about politics. You're either brave or stupid... my mom will eat you alive once she gets out of the shower. She informs herself. Just look at her history books." She pointed at the bookshelf. There were very few fiction books. The bulk of her repertoire was history and political science.

"She's read all of that?" I asked in astonishment.

"Oh yeah, and that doesn't include what she's been getting from the library over the years. When she gets financially defunct, she runs off to the library and brings back book after book about Marx and Engels."

***

Ami was not exaggerating, Minerva was a brilliant woman,

highly educated in the academes, and she knew what she was talking about, especially when it came to politics. And Ami was just as vociferous and strident, so I listened as closely as I could...

Within two minutes, she had me completely absorbed. Before this conversation, I'd never really taken much interest in politics, other than a few books here and there. I thought it was nothing more than two disagreeing horsemen on the same horse, heading in the same direction though they oblige their differences as oblique. And to a certain extent, she agreed with me when I said that, but it was so much more complicated than this, as she advised me.

"What you have to understand," she said as the three of us sat at the kitchen table, "is that Lenin, Stalin, Mao, and Hitler completely distorted Marx's ideas. Socialism is about social and financial equality, not pogroms and conquest. Mankind can't have justice until there's equality, there's no getting passed it. Based on the current GDP, each citizen in the US would get approximately $52,000 per year per capita... that's $1000 per week. It's more than enough to survive on..."

"And, of course," Ami said, "what my mother neglects to mention yet again, is that the dictator of this political system has absolute power over everyone and everything that happens in the country: from the media to the economy. 'Power corrupts; and absolute power corrupts absolutely.' You've heard it a thousand times but it's true, isn't it? Opposition has to develop underground because there's no political opposition to be had, no possibility for reform whatsoever---Pravda. You want to live in a dictatorship? I've heard hundreds of stories about people trying to escape Communism in dingy boats made of trash. Why do you believe in dictatorship? It's crazy! Communism stagnates your potential. Look at what's happening in Venezuela right now, after seventeen-years of Socialism: all the shelves in the grocery stores are completely empty, and they have armed guards in front of each isle to ensure that people don't take too much of this or that according to their rations. You have to wait in line for eight hours just to get some fucking rice from the Government. No Soya sauce, by the way. No Soya sauce. Even electricity and toilet paper are rationed by the Government. So if you run out, you run out for the rest of the month, and you can't even wipe your ass. Money there is absolutely worthless… you can't even buy a loaf of bread with a suitcase full of money because of hyperinflation… the more money you print the less it's worth. Everybody knows that, and that's why Socialism always fails and turns into anarchy. People are even starting to disappear, which can only mean one things: they're being put into concentration camps. And now there are thousands of FEMA camps in North America. The Government says that it's for national emergencies and disasters. But if that's true, why are they surrounded by barbed wire? That's because they want to do the same thing here in America that they did in Venezuela for the New World Order. Let us all traipse to the gulag like good citizens… Sounds wonderful!"

"Why would you want to reform equality? Socialism doesn't prevent anyone from living their lives. It's just complacency, that's all. If you're complacent, everything's fine. In a free society, everything should be free! Movies, cars, books, the bus, education, health care… everything!"

Ami rebuked her and said: "To work without getting paid is the definition of slavery… That's Communism! It's evil! Its like national welfare for all the provosts. It takes away your ambition, there's simply nothing to accomplish except for its own sake, so why do it…? We're human, we need an incentive to work… to succeed, we need freedom in order to be happy. Do you want a 90% tax? What we need to do as a society is establish a Government website where everyone votes on everything: from minimum wage to abortion to tax reform. Absolutely everything. That way the Government would yield its power completely to the people: it wouldn't matter who's in charge, because of the people would be in charge. They would indict their own will on the system instead of the other way around… it would be like total democracy."

I could tell they'd had this conversation before. Minerva turned to me again. "Do you know how many people in this dear country of ours have to work two or three jobs just to survive? Solomon, forgive Ami. She doesn't know what she's talking about. She's pretty but her mind's been on vacation for years; she's forgotten what it's like to toil rationally. I'm fully convinced that if the Government found out the true meaning of my paintings they would drag me out of here and throw me in prison without a peep. But politicians aren't subjective enough to understand art. I have a friend. His name is Pavlov and he used to be a spy---"

"He used to be a spy and he told you this?" I said.

"Yes... He resigned after he was assigned to stash some drugs in the house of a known socialist just so they could keep his political insight undercover. Pavlov wrote a book about his time as a spy and guess what? They censored it---they halted its publication and banned it from libraries and schools, because they don't want the citizens of this country to know the truth."

"Yeah," Ami said, "because it would obviously be a matter of national security."

"Oh, that's just the line they keep using because no one wants to traduce something as logically impossible as national security. The fact is, if someone decides to blow up a building with his car, who's going to stop him? But it's pretty convenient to keep people afraid and on the edge all the fucking time. Do you think politicians are somehow unaware that people are at their most patriotic when they are under threat? Hello-o! Have you ever heard of 'A People's History of the United States,' by Howard Zinn?"

Ami said: "I haven't read that one yet. But I know who he is and what he's about. He told me about that book…"

"It's about America's history, not from the point of view of politicians, but from the point of view of actual citizens. It's from 1492 to the present. On the very first page, he quotes a log kept by Columbus before and after his 'discovery.' Columbus goes on to describe how the Arawaks looked, how shapely they were, how they dressed. Then he says this: 'They do not bear arms, and they not know them, for I showed them a sword, they took it by the edge and cut themselves out of ignorance. They have no iron. Their spears are made of cane... They would make fine servants... With fifty men, we could subjugate them all and make them do whatever we want.' And they did just that, they would force the Arawaks to go into the hills and mountains and rivers and search for gold. If you came back with some, they gave you a copper necklace and you were fine, but if you failed, they would cut off your hands and let you bleed to death on the shore. But, of course, they don't teach that in history classes." She looked at Ami. "Is this the kind of Democracy that you're talking about?"

Ami rolled her eyes. "So Columbus was full of shit... okay... fine. That doesn't denote the idea of Democracy that people should be free to choose their own modus operandi... their own destiny under the stakes of a free country."

I loved it when Ami talked like an intellectual... she was so goddamn pedantic, like a dilettante on Ritalin...

"Free? Freedom is just a sales pitch for uninformed people too busy with their social lives to care about the truth. The fact is, if we want a healthy society, we have to treat it like a body; certain things have to be banished, cut off like a gangrenous limb...."

"Like what?" I asked.

"Smoking, pornography, tuition; any Capitalist sensationalism that creates addictions and financial depression. It creates a polemic cycle for us proles... and it's never going to stop so long as you live, Solomon."

"Well," Ami said, "if I could sum you up in one word, mom, it would be 'naïve.'"

"I for one love naïve people, because, whatever you have to say about naiveté... it's always more educated than apathy." She smiled at her own wit.

Ami looked at me and said, "Are you a socialist yet...?" She looked at her watch. "We better get going if we're going to make the movie."

I looked at my watch. It was 6:31 PM... the movie was at seven o'clock. The real reason for getting out of there was to go smoke some reefer with Ami's friend. She got pretty wild when she was high. She would start talking about the most random things. It was hilarious.

***

After the matinee movie, we left and went to her sister's duplex down the street. She greeted us at the door and took us to her basement. Her father loved Pink Floyd, and had painted the room like the cover of his favourite album, "Dark Side of the Moon." The prism on a black background…

Her sister was great at rolling joints, and so she usually did it for us. With two reefer sticks ashen and taking affect, we started talking. The conversation was just as erratic as usual, mostly because of Ami.

She looked at us and kind of chuckled. "You know what would be really cool? If time travel were possible…"

"That's crazy…" I just said.

"Well…" Ami began. "There's this scientist who thinks he knows how to time travel. He wants to use Einstein's theory to bend space. And, according to the theory, if you can bend space somehow, time bends with it, because they're two-in-one. So, yeah, this guy might be time traveling pretty soon. Who am I to talk about that…? After all, I failed physics twice in high school…"

I said: "Hey, if you could talk to either your future self or your past self, who would you talk to…"

Ami said: "I would talk to my future self…"

"I would talk to my past self, just to tell myself that things are going to get better… also I'd like to warn people about a few things so that they don't happen… like 9/11… I'd also like to experience the 60s for myself…" I paused." Ok, let's put on some music… how about 'The Doors?'"

"How about some Solomon Roy…?" Ami said jokingly.

"Hahaha… I'm not even close to being finished writing my album…"

"So play it live… play !Okarma! for us. Pleeeease…"

"No way… you know how shy I am about my music, Ami… forget it."

CHAPTER FIVE

I know I don't have to tell you this by now, but Ami was very cynical about politics: like a desensitized goddess on acid---an agnostic angel on aspartame.

I was in love with Ami Eston from head to toe. It was like a sacrilege of dioptres in my soul, frittering in dribs and drabs, as an ideal and nothing more---a drop in the ocean, which yet consumes it.

She was feeling particularly self-righteous, so she went to her CD collection and put on some carefully selected music---John Lennon's "Imagine," the album---one of my all-time favourites. She sang along like an out of tune record player---obviously on purpose. She had a great singing voice, like a honey-tongued seraphim, but she was so high that she forgot half the words, and this, for some reason, made her laugh even more.

This caused me to have one of those moments when you look at a girl, and she doesn't know you love her. I looked at her laughing, and I just wanted to kiss her, or at least, hold her in my arms on the divan in the corner next to the surround sound. Finally, she looked at me and asked me what my problem was. I think she knew. She knew that I loved her. I could tell by her deportment and her carriage when she was around me. I was enthralled... and totally engrossed by her personage, even by her grandee.

To me, she was like Dominique Swain in "Lolita," she was so beautiful and innocent to me. I just couldn't resist her raw sexuality, and her flirtation... and I said nothing to protrude it. You see, poets tend to fall in love more deeply than the rest of us...

Ami suddenly jumped up and started dancing like a nymph in a discotheque, a raggedy puppet on a stage. Girls are like that--- spontaneous and crazy. It was spur-of-the-moment, I suppose; and I loved every minute of it. I was thoroughly captivated by her spontaneity. With every move she made, I fell deeper and deeper into the arroyo that would swallow my mind and soul for months to come. But, of course, I didn't want her to know about this. It was my little secret to keep… like a Pandora's box in reverse.

Love tends to immolate your modesty with a quick fire in the mind and the soul.

"She eyes me like a Pisces when I am weak…"

***

When I returned home, the apartment was silent---too silent. To my horror, my mother had finally succeeded in taking her own life---she was overdosed on the floor, her mouth agape and frothing, her hair dishevelled, her expression spread out like an open conch withholding the sea---that I finally understood the mortar of her disease. I felt so desperately alone from that moment on that life to me seemed like nothing more than an impossible trial of the will, and my perception of God was scornful to the point of denial---even hatred against myself.

As I kneeled next to her, weeping like a child overwhelmed with the strange contagion of disbelief, everything became surreal... There was no traffic outside, there were no windows to the world, there was nothing else except this moment. And all I could do was weep and let my tears fall on my mother's rigid, lilac face. My mother's death confirmed my perception of life: that it was absurd, ugly, and sardonic. So I started doing a lot more drugs to alleviate my pain…

"And me happiest when I'm high…"

***

Ami kept trying to contact me on Facebook, but I ignored her. I didn't want to hear her sympathy or her condolences. I didn't want to hear anyone say that they were sorry for me, or that they understood what I was going through, because, the truth was, they couldn't possibly know what it felt like to be me at that particular time. I didn't even get to say goodbye to her, or how much I loved her.

***

I was going off to live with my father. I thought it would be especially nice to see my older brother again. He was studying philosophy and literature at Yale as an Ivy League student. His professor was none other than Harold Bloom, my all-time favourite critic. I'd read "Genius," "The Western Canon," "How to Read and Why," and "Shakespeare: The Invention of the Human."

I wanted to show him my work… but it wasn't quite ready yet.

I remember I showed my poetry to my mother when I was sixteen, and she was convinced that I had stolen it from T.S. Eliot---there was no way I could write like that at that age, or any age for that matter. She always said that I was an old-soul.

Metempsychosis…

***

I didn't realize how much my life would change. I'd gone through some pretty swift changes in my life: with fleets of distain and amnesia, combined into a kind of intellectual pomade. Moving to Greenwich Village when I was twelve had taught me a lot about urban life: Greenwich Village had a culture of its own, its own dialcct, its own colloquialism if you will. It had cvcrything you could possibly imagine---every possible business for every possible person. It was nothing less than a Mecca for Capitalism…

My father also lived at the center of the creative world as an avant-garde Rodin-like sculptor. I often went to The Café Wha? to write my opus, which was loosely based on my life, as you will see… That's also where Bob Dylan got known before he met John Hammond, the man who signed him to Columbia Records. My brother once took me to the pub where Dylan used to play---the Gaslight Café.

It was closed now, but it was still pretty cool to see it.

He also took me to the spot where Lennon was shot and where

the city made a memorial for him, where people gathered to mourn his death. None of this livened up my spirits, though. I only had two things in mind, my mother and Ami. They had been my two biggest influences.

I found out a lot about my father while I stayed with him. It turned out he liked the same music I did. And he had his own stash of reefer in a tin can, too. His knowledge spanned mostly across the plains of music history. He would say stuff like: "You know the literal street meaning of rock'n'roll is 'sex and drugs.' Those Negroes at the time put a slant on everything they said. Some-times I wish I would been a black man, then I could've played like the greats, Desmond Dekker, Muddy Waters, Louis Armstrong, Ike Turner." My father was a great guitar player. He loved jazz and the blues but he could play in any style.

Most of the time we spent together, we were high. I tried to introduce him to Absinthe, but he took one sip and looked at me like I was crazy.

"Is it supposed to taste like black liquorice?" he asked.

"Yeah… You get used to it after a while. I drink it because it's what all the old artists used to drink for inspiration. Name a great artist, chances are they drank this stuff regularly. Vincent van Gogh, Picasso, Oscar Wilde, Charles Baudelaire, Hemingway, Rimbaud, Poe, Verlaine…"

***

I remember, my guitar teacher, Jacque, after listening to my album !OKARMA! for the first time, said that the world wasn't ready for a real artist, and that I was overestimating the intelligence of my audience by 1000%. I didn't want to believe it at first, but the more I thought about it, the more it made sense to me…

We are literally being dumbed down by the U.S. government to accept the New World Order, but I am here to turn the tide… I don't care how much I have to suffer to speak the rite against the Postmodernist digerati… depending, of course, on their critique.

I, on the other hand, loved real artists, so I would often visit the

Museum of Modern Art---MoMA---and I looked at van Gogh's "The Starry Night" for a while---among others. Sometimes, my dad would derail me and call me a monk. He would ask me if I wanted some aconite for my pipe. Aconite was this Old World drug found in monkshood plants. My father was clever like that with puns. Sometimes he was so clever I didn't catch his drift at all and the things he said just went right over my head. My brother was really book smart, so I took to his philosophies like an ayatollah. Everything he said made so much sense to me. He knew about eastern religions, European philosophers, all sorts of writers. He was a Buddhist, a vegetarian, and an opium addict. His favourite writer was George Orwell; his favourite spiritual teacher was some guru named Osho from India; his favourite philosopher was Hobbes, just like me. We mostly talked about spiritual things, though. We didn't go much into politics. He would mostly negate the whole idea of politics as a plenum where wisdom has no seat, or as a means to put progress on a treadmill. When something would pop up on the tube, he'd say something like: 'This is exactly the kind of language Orwell talked about, Solomon. It's designed to make lies sound truthful, murder respectable, and to give the appearance of solidity to pure wind.'

"One guy says the education system needs reforms that will increase inner-city grades, and the other guy says the education system needs total refinement to instigate African-Americans to rise to the occasion of their manifest destiny, even as it goes against manifest destiny's precepts. It's the same implication with different words. There's no real debate here, Solomon. It's just the implication of a debate. It has a stage, podiums, and rich politicians, who don't know what it feels like to eat at a soup kitchen let alone how to stabilize the economic system. That's the thing about this Capitalist mindset that we have; it's all about making as much money as possible, but even as our salaries get higher, so does the summit of our desires and needs. The more you make, the more you spend; the more you spend, the more you need. I'll tell you what the irony of our economy is: rich people have a far greater debt to society than the poor. We're getting pretty close to Christmas, but I don't think even one percent of this country could even begin to tell you how this tradition started."

"How did it start then?"

"There was this old guy, a patron saint, who would go across the Netherlands on a boat and would deliver presents to children to celebrate the birth of Christ. The countrymen loved him so much that they brought him along with them to the new found land of America. They founded a city called New Amsterdam, which then adopted the name of New York. And the old guy's name changed from Sinter Klaus to Santa Claus. Then in the twentieth century, a really pure-hearted company called Coca-Cola took this legend and expanded its commercial value by giving him a red suit, a long beard and jolly red cheeks to help sell their product to children, because they understood that the whole point of Christmas was to take advantage of their ignorance, since they want everything they see, and the image of Santa Claus just entices them to the boiling point. Isn't it amazing? The whole function of society is to subjugate us to become comp-lacent citizens with big, fat wallets and empty souls. The more spiritually defunct society becomes, the more we'll look in material things to fill that void." He paused and turned off the television. "Do you know who T.S Eliot is?"

"Yeah, but I don't know much about him."

"April is the cruellest month…? You should really read up on his poetry. Especially 'The Waste Land.' It perfectly limns out what I'm talking about. Everyday, I walk these streets and all I see is oblivious people with the strange idea that life needs to have a schedule, a structure, a routine. It's like a voluntary prison for the involuntary mind, the id. And unless you're some sort of anarchist, you just wake up everyday and live out the exact same process with only a few discrepancies to keep you sane."

***

After he finished his discourse, I went out for a walk. It had become a part of my daily routine. I would go to the bookstore, the record store, grab a cup of coffee at Starbucks, and then go back home to listen to the album or read the books I bought. But today, something strange happened. At first, I thought I was just being paranoid, but as I kept walking, even as I changed my usual route, my paranoia seemed to be justified. I was being followed. The culprit was a strange man in a black overcoat and a black hat. He looked like he had walked straight out of the fifties.

So I changed my routine a bit to see if he would follow me. I went to the park to read my book, and this man, without hesitation, sat directly next to me. He sparked a cigarillo. He then asked me if I wanted one. I ignored him and started wondering if I should walk away. But before I could, he said something that changed my life forever.

He said, "How long has it been, Solomon?"

I closed my book and tried to get a good look at his face. "How do you know my name?"

"You don't remember me?" He smiled slightly. He puffed and puffed on his cigarette. Then he said: "You had such a vision of the street as the street hardly understands. " He looked at me and winked. "Sound familiar?"

That was from a T.S Eliot poem. Sometimes things happen in such a way that you can't help but be suspicious about reality. My brother had brought up the same poet only a few hours before.

"Yeah, it does sound familiar... Sounds like Eliot."

"It is Eliot. My personal favourite. I used to quote him to you all the time, along with a few others, of course."

He took off his hat, revealing an old face with wise, smiling eyes. It was Mr. Jones, my English teacher from High School. He had introduced me to real literature, like Shakespeare and Dante. He had given me a copy of Bloom's "Genius" when I was seventeen. I didn't recognize him because of his beard and glasses. He had been almost everyone's favourite teacher. He was by far the most know-ledgeable man I had ever known.

He had been all over the world to learn about linguistics, astronomy, physics, art, music, and anything else you can think of. He was in search of wisdom, not just knowledge. I had tried many times to determine the difference, and came up with my own ideas about it. I thought knowledge was more based on facts and figures, while wisdom is a little bit less tangible. Wisdom is what experience has taught you; it's the omniscient light in each of us that rids us of all forms of darkness. One of my favourite lines in "The Catcher in the Rye" seemed to resound the same theme. I don't remember it, so I'll just paraphrase: "The immature man looks for a cause to die for; while the mature man looks for a cause to live for." That's why I love that book. I just don't understand why all those crazy people burnt it. People always burn the best books. If I ever write one, I hope they burn it, because that'll just mean it was provocative, like all great art should be.

Sometimes, the best way to get through to people is by insulting their intelligence. I don't mean to say that they're ignorant, but that there's things the mind can't grasp under its social conditioning sometimes. Like when a man walks into a store and buys all sorts of clothes for his family, but he doesn't know that the people who fabricate his luxuries work in these sweatshops for eighty cents a day. Not that it makes a difference in the end, but that it's better to build up your compassion and be broke than to become a complete asshole about everything and think the world revolves around your own ideas.

Anyway, as I sat there with Mr. Jones, I couldn't help but think about everything that had happened to me. I thought I had finally found someone to guide me. I wanted to spend as much time with him as possible, so I had to find out what he was doing in New York. He said, "Well, Solomon, I'm a Professor of English Literature at Yale. Mostly Shakespeare..."

"That's where my brother goes. Is he in one of your classes?"

"Yes... Actually, he is in one of my classes... My Shakespeare class."

"That's crazy."

"Life keeps its secrets well, doesn't it? No one knows if everything is prerequisite or just about as random as the zephyr. Maybe God's got such a hold on us that we don't even know it. But I think you have to ask first."

"Yeah, maybe I should... My faith kind of fluctuates sometimes. "

"Oh, it's like that for everyone, Solomon. Mother Teresa doubted God for fifty years. But she kept doing her work, though. In the end that's all that matters; that you just kept on going even when everything was telling you to stop." He paused. "What do you say we go to my apartment? I've got some books I want you to read."

"All right... what books?"

"You'll see when we get there. I have a few in mind that I think you might like…"

He ended up giving me a copy of "1984," by George Orwell, and a copy of "Brave New World," by Aldous Huxley.

These books would ruin my life…

CHAPTER SIX

My mother had always been obsessed with the Freemasons and the New World Order, as well as the Illuminati, which is apparently hand in glove.

She even showed me once that if you go to a website whose address is Illuminati spelled backwards (www.itanimulli.com), it takes you to the U.S. Government's National Security website...

The Illuminati is a group that, for hundreds of years, has dictated the fate of the world---modern-day Rosicrucians. If you've never read "Atlas Shrugged" by Ayn Rand, I suggest you do so as soon as possible, especially if you're a Libertarian like me. It's about a man who attempts to stop the motor of the world by being an individual amongst the collective, as well as his vernacular as a man.

Apparently, the Illuminati told Ayn Rand to write her novel as a blue-collar manual for their plans of world domination---a global enclave of Socialism under the reign of the Antichrist. If you can picture Atlas holding the globe and shrugging, you would be right to assume that the world's axis would shift into a paradigm. This has already happened, and things are progressing according to plan.

Now, if you have a dollar bill on you, I suggest you look at it as you read on. Notice on the reverse the All-seeing eye above the pyramid? This is in reference to Big Brother---the CEO of America. They see or will eventually see everything we do, as it was suggested in Orwell's "1984." Beneath the pyramid are the words NOVUS ORDO SECLORUM---New World Order. This is the Illuminati's manifest destiny: 1776.

Now, the words above the pyramid: ANNUIT COEPTIS--- God has approved of our beginnings.

That was the Freemasons... they control everything, using symbols and sigils everywhere in society, like a corporate pyramid. And this is how my journey began to oblate them to the populace...

My mother once told me that all these multinational corporations that have the number 666 in their emblem, are corporations owned and operated by Freemasons and/or the Illuminati.

She figured this out by determining that the number 666 is in the Disney World's emblem, due in large part to the fact that Walt Disney was an avid Freemason…

Also, if you've ever seen the statue of George Washington in the Washington D.C., you'll notice that he is in the exact same position as Baphomet in that famous Masonic drawing…

Also, the symbol of Baphomet is embroidered into the hats of Freemasons for the three higher degrees, like a triple cross.

These people are hiding in plain sight… controlling the world behind the shadows like puppeteers.

It was one hell of a conspiracy… but I believed it to be true.

***

I was now living on my own at Hotel Chelsea with my inheritance. I had even brought my BOSS BR-1200 to record, mix, and master my album: !OKARMA!... It's about the death of Postmodernism, and the birth of Metamodernism. !OKARMA! was a literary pastiche about society as I saw it---a burlesque about my personal lingo, which was also in sync with the "Wizard of Oz."

All in all, it's a caveat for the Illuminati, a "Death Certificate" for those who refuse to bow down to God, so watch it circumspectly for yourself. There's a political message, but there's also a spiritual message written specifically for the brethren, so listen closely to the lyrics even as you peruse the film as a background to its augury… with synchronicity from beginning to end: word per word, and lyric per lyric...

I'm actually using their own movie against them. "The Wizard of Oz" is obviously Masonic from beginning to end: the path to illumination---it's downright Luciferian.

Meanwhile, here are the lyrics in full:

1. !OKARMA! (3:36)
2. ECLECTIC HOODOO MAN (3:42)
3. POSTMODERN MAGDALENE* (3:56)
4. (… THE CRYSTAL BALL…) (3:12)
5. SOLONS IN DYSTOPIA (3:01)
6. THE EGYPTIAN OZ (4:03)
7. CYCLOPS INC. (2:34)
8. A BRIEF HISTORY OF TIME (4:44)
9. THE SHAPE-SHIFTER (2:40)
10. MR.CATCH-22 (2:12)
11. SHANGRI-LA'S LOT (3:17)
12. PRE-MADONNA* (3:35)
13. STARS-OF-BETHLEHEM (3:34)
14. EAST OF EDEN (…)
15. ILLUMINATION 4:20 (…)
16. DEAR PIANOMAN (…)
17. CATCHER IN THE RYE (…)
18. SUMMER OF LOVE: 1967* (…)
19. BUSINESS MONKEY* (…)
20. CITY OF THE DAMNED (…)
21. STAIRWAY TO HELL (…)
22. FASCIST RADIO NWO (…)
23. APOLLO'S WAKE (7:37)

!OKARMA! is in sync with "The Wizard of Oz."
For the full anti-Illuminati experience, make sure the first lyric
starts at the exact moment you see the intro: "For nearly forty years…"
(This album is about Judy Garland*… who died of an overdose in 1969.)
The Illuminati is real, and it's everywhere.

!OKARMA!

Okarma, why did you forsake me?
You drove me out of spirits
And cast lots for my garments…
Okarma, the Holy Ghost is gone,
And fate's just got no pity
For things you choose to die for…

My karma's got me inside out,
Feeling like a lazy diamond stuck in
Vanilla Skies… Vanilla Skies…

Okarma, I tried to wash your sins away,
But dirty thoughts always won you over,
Always won you over…
Okarma, your freedom's got no choice now,
You're breaking bread with a dying man,
Breaking bread with a dying man…

My karma's got me inside out,
Feeling like a lazy diamond stuck in
Vanilla Skies… Vanilla Skies…

I got stuck in the easy way out,
I got stuck the easy way out…
My world's turning black and white,
An "invisible man" stuck on easy street.
I got stuck in the easy way out,
I got stuck in the easy way out…
My world's turning black and white,
My dreams never took to the "klieg light."

My karma's got me inside out,
Feeling like a lazy diamond stuck in
Vanilla Skies… Vanilla Skies…

My karma's got me inside out,
Feeling like a lazy diamond stuck in
Vanilla Skies… Vanilla Skies…

ECLECTIC HOODOO MAN

There's a Hoodoo Man down on easy street,
Nine subconscious hells lay beneath his feet.
When the sundown melts to black,
Good ole karma gets you back.
Don't let the rising Sun deceive you, dear,
No one talks about the darkness here,
'til it looms above your head,
Leaves your angels noosed and dead.

When the weather's in your head,
Just numb your senses like you do.
When your dreams bode what you dread,
Just numb your senses like you do…

Make your way uptown to the Miser's Inn,
Where good people go to damn their sins.
But the Devil knows your ways,
And your bright side never stays.
Every doorway leads you to a secret room;
You must close your eyes or watch your doom.
If you stay there's dreams to find,
If you leave you'll lose your mind.

When the weather's in your head,
Just numb your senses like you do.
When your dreams bode what you dread,
Just numb your senses like you do…
Like you do…

Again… you will never feel again…
Again… you will never feel again…
Your consumption will consume you,
And your presumption will presume you (dead).
You will never feel again…

A "klieg light" is shining from the sky down to the ground;
It gleams without a sound.
The future is looking like the past in a telltale light,
Your mind is out of sight…

POSTMODERN MAGDALENE*

There's no Elysium in her eyes,
The taste of life's like wine;
She says it's bittersweet.
She thinks her body's made of dust,
To dust she must return;
Lest secrets let her out.
She feels so good sometimes it hurts me
To brood upon her flesh
As if there's nothing else…

*When she breaks into a song,
Her people sing along…
And then she says: "I'm not your baby."
But when she finally takes too much
She'll know she's out of touch
And float above the airwaves.*

When there's a séance in her mind,
She seeks the looking-glass
And sees herself look back.
She lights the incense on her desk
And smokes up in her room;
The world just disappears.
I do my best not to abet her,
She tells me not to care;
Proviso's got no choice…

*When she breaks into a song,
Her people sing along…
And then she says: "I'm not your baby."
But when she finally takes too much
She'll know she's out of touch
And float above the airwaves.*

A white noise euphonium was playing on the stereo,
The room turned to spirals made of sound.
She died in the magazines, Postmodern Magdalene;
Fought with her silence 'til it broke her spirit…

The rooms aroma smells like sex,
Just can't dispel the hex,
That leads her lies astray.
I feel like clay that's turned to dust,
My marrow soon will rust,
For me there's nothing else.
My better angels got the worst of me;
My spirit's spiraling down,
Proviso's got not choice…

(…war doc on the television…)

(…THE CRYSTAL BALL…)

(Instrumental)

SOLONS IN DYSTOPIA

Your life's a waking dream,
A silver screen's subconscious light.
Don't matter what it means,
'Cause all you see's in black and white.

"I know, the Devil keeps you down within your thoughts;
Replaces you with someone that you are not."

You tried to talk some sense,
But no one heard just what you meant.
Don't buy this fib's intents,
It speaks of things you've never dreamt.

"I know, naivety's got nothing on its mind;
I'll teach you not to seek what you cannot find."

There's a black cloud in city hall
That drowns the town's cerulean skies.
If you want to see the fall,
Just wait until the weather dies.

"I know, it's hard to keep your mind when nothing's found;
You'll drive out all your demons with a silver sound."

THE EGYPTIAN OZ

Cinema graphic angels in my room,
The white visitation bends my walls.
Time is warped to the nth degree of space;
The left dimension opens up before me.

Somnambulate through meadows made of gold,
Lead me on to the Ancient Days of Old.
A brass snake that eats itself at the tail,
Weaves a spell like a queen beneath a veil.

Tornadoes tore Kansas apart,
And space-time just drifted apart,
It feels like a dream but it's not,
And now you must find what you sought.

In the land of Oz there are people in the trees,
A mawkin made of straw portends their fate.
If Eden's lost in the apple of my eye,
The electrum angel's scepter would resolve me.

The zodiac child is asleep on empty air,
Dreaming dreams Egyptians never dare.
The wishing well is a portal to the past,
The feeling's good but the feeling never lasts.

Tornadoes tore Kansas apart,
And space-time just drifted apart,
It feels like a dream but it's not,
And now you must find what you sought.

Tornadoes tore Kansas apart,
And space-time just drifted apart,
It feels like a dream but it's not,
And now you must find what you sought.

(Tornadoes tore Kansas apart,
And space-time just drifted apart,
It feels like a dream but it's not,
And now you must find what you sought.)

CYCLOPS INC.

If you think you've got "secrets" take a deeper look at mine:
Seems my life is just a dream from the one-eyed man.
No, we won't meet again until our fates do intertwine,
Until the music puts a trance on the fields of Pan.

Sounds like you've got something to hide,
Something to hide...

So wipe those tears away, 'cause they're the last you'll ever drop;
And make a pledge that you will try to know my stops.
Take my palm in hand and we'll never be apart,
Until the love of God aspires from jovial hearts.

Sounds like you've got something to hide,
Something to hide...

Undecided and regressive to your stare,
So desperate to break free but I never dare.
Fill the 'darkling glass' with the third eye in your mind,
To turn the Cyclops into sand... 'cause he's out of time.

A BRIEF HISTORY OF TIME

You who turns the wheel of time, look onward, you've seen everything
And you know karma's olden soul will sing.
As Hell's abyss surrounds my mind, belief strings aphoristic men
To handless thoughts that hold on to their Zen.
As fate sends gamblers to the slaves, they gamble for each others' graves,
But never seem to realize what it staves.
I saw the Hoodoo Man's prognosis diving down to lovers' dreams,
He told me that it's never what it seems…
But in these times of "War and Peace" I humble kings to honour thieves,
And give them back the freedoms love achieves.
I know your gold means so much more, than dying on a gypsy's floor,
With spans of conscience greater when you're poor.
But when the poor man's fate reveals the image of your vanities,
Compassion earns a glance but never sees.
I saw a god man crucified: a Calvary up on Caesar's knolls,
He even spoke forgiveness to their souls.
The Miser's Inn, the silent halls, directed me to heed the call,
Of echoes that my mind could not recall.
I issued poltroons to the thrones and told them "understand your mind,
You've given all your riches to your kind…"
Behind the doors on either side, I thought I heard your mysteries died:
Too little to reveal, too much to hide.
The answer hides inside and dies of truth, of pain whose aught collides,
Like cosmic ghosts that haunt the midst of ides…
You found your psalms in Kansas dreams, I heard you cry in orchid steam,
You sat there like a monk within my dream.
The Hoodoo Man died yesterday, and I, in my own crazy faith,
Must say that faith's like needles in a wraith…
'Cause you who've seen the dreams of time, your memoirs left no paradigms,
The wheel keeps moving on despite your rimes.
Your pain is just a liar that keeps time and says: "Your soul is mine!"
The less you know the less you earned your mind.
I've challenged fools to games of chess, the stalemates left me to profess:
"You equal what you judge without redress…"
And so I've seen these kismets glow: primordial karma's on a rood,
He died there with his mind misunderstood.
Claims to know you head to toe, a prophet on 'Desolation Row,'
His eloquence still begs you to bestow.
It's not just how the music flows, it's how your prescience will implode
When music dies and heaven hears your ode…

THE SHAPE-SHIFTER

Your heart's meant to slow you down,
Whenever your thoughts turn your smile to a frown.
Your mind is a dreamscape out of town,
Where Jane Seymour's ghost wears a pearl studded crown.
Your Dark Side, her Highness, is aloof,
She squawks like a 'cat on a hot tin roof.'
It's less of a nightmare than you think;
It's not like you ran out of ink…

Just leave it alone,
Just leave it alone
And you'll find your way home…
Just leave it alone,
Just leave it alone
And you'll find your way home…

Sleep like a baby in a shawl,
She'll play with your fear like a Camorra doll.
So follow your instinct like a "star,"
You'll never be free if you stay where you are.
You hide in your telltale heart,
And "shift into shape" to get back to the start.
Get back to the yellow brick road,
And sing that melodious ode…

Just leave it alone,
Just leave it alone
And you'll find your way home…
Just leave it alone,
Just leave it alone
And you'll find your way home…

(…)

"Here lieth a Phoenix, by whose death
Another Phoenix life gave breath:
It is to be lamented much
The world at once ne'er knew two such.

MR. CATCH-22

Always caught up in a "no-mind" situation,
Sounds like there's a stranger in your brain.
Stuck in a 'self-defeating course of action,'
If you catch his drift it'll make you sane.

Mister Catch . . . Mister Catch . . . Mister Catch-22.
Mister Catch . . . Mister Catch . . . Mister Catch-22.

Hanging out on Fleet Street when the weather's meet,
He reconnoiters every cloud like atomic rain.
It's not the time of day that makes your sugar (LSD) sweet,
There's no use in explaining when it's vain.

Mister Catch . . . Mister Catch . . . Mister Catch-22.
Mister Catch . . . Mister Catch . . . Mister Catch-22.

There's a swan song satellite that sings to you,
State of mind shuts you down when you know too much.
It's a stranger's paradise when the liar's you,
Too many mistakes in the common touch.

Mister Catch . . . Mister Catch . . . Mister Catch-22.
Mister Catch . . . Mister Catch . . . Mister Catch-22.

SHANGRI-LA'S LOT

It seems redundant
To wallow in your sin,
'Cause time will follow you,
No matter where you've been…

The Devil sees in black and white,
An Orpheus "klieg light" …
Can't travel through time if it slows you down,
If it's inside out you must be in a ghost town…

If what I seek is lost in you,
You'll find your pride runs through and through…
Let's take our souls to invisible spaces
And take our lot to Shangri-la…

You're not God's automaton,
With pulsars in your snare.
Would you double dare me
To tell you that he'll be there…?

When heaven sleeps it dreams of this,
But you'd never notice…
It dawns on everybody if it's true,
So don't think twice if it tries to get to you…

If what I seek is lost in you,
You'll find remorse runs through and through…
Let's take our souls to invisible spaces
And take our lot to Shangri-la…

PRE-MADONNA*
(…prima donna…)

Lost pre-Madonna girl keeps thinking
'bout the "monkey on her back,"
Find a fix until she's broken,
'til her cancer turns to black.
"Snake in the grass" to say sex sells
but money never tells a lie,
And Mary-Jane just makes me smile
when she's bi…

*Spiral down
to the subtle side of life.
Beneath the surface of your mind
you'll find no strife.
Take your time and give it space
to let affinities begin,
The mirrors in your mind will
multiply themselves
without an end…*

Black cherry schoolgirl keeps on
waiting for the Devil to come out,
Could never tell if Hell is down
beneath the shadow of a doubt.
Either way it's just a dream
until reality sets in;
Eat the apple, shut your mouth
and make me sin…

*Spiral down
to the subtle side of life.
Beneath the surface of your mind
you'll find no strife.
Take your time and give it space
to let affinities begin,
The mirrors in your mind will
multiply themselves
without an end…*

Crawl down the rabbit-hole and fall

through time and space straight down to Hell,
Is this the end of time, is this the place
Mephisto spoke his spell?
The daemons in your head will swear
unto the day they take your stead,
Let the Devil find his way
back to your bed…

Spiral down
to the subtle side of life.
Beneath the surface of your mind
you'll find no strife.
Take your time and give it space
to let affinities begin,
The mirrors in your mind will
multiply themselves…
without an end…
without an end…
without an end…
without an end…

STARS-OF-BETHLEHEM

Once upon a time you knew just who you were;
No dishonesty, no mystery in your heart of hearts.
Now you make your mind do things it shouldn't do;
Hard to tell if what you say is ever true to you.

Silver-tongued without a heart to speak from,
Simple-minded ends don't know where to begin again.
False to falser, falsest is still yet to come;
Puppeteer without a puppet strung to hyper-Zen.
Made-up wisdom takes its secrets to the grave;
Free will never wills its freedom to another slave.

Free the slaves, enslave the free,
And blind the insights that you see.
Find excuses to excuse
The lack of judgment that you use.
Aspire to no one else but you
That you alone might make it through.
Need your wonts and wont your needs,
To kill the ego that it feeds.

"Reign of Terror" from a castle made of sand;
Simian outlaws, stalking angels, traipsing hand to hand.
Pray that love can break a heart made out of stone;
Stars-of-Bethlehem will fall on empty headstones.
Feeling good is just effect without the cause,
Spreading sunlight with no Sun into the heliopause.

Tired of the same old story line,
Tired of the same old, same old... (x 2)

EAST OF EDEN

PART I

East of Eden there's a silver light
That leads the souls of men to stray,
Where ghetto angels don't believe in sight,
And what they do see, they won't say…
A flaming sword keeps out the sinners and their sin,
Repartees left and right: the doors at Miser's Inn;
So winnow grain from chaff, partake 'em to get high:
Failures fail and fail to try…

East of Eden there's a yellow road,
That leads your soul through vogues and gleams;
Intone along to every liar's node;
Passions made in a dead man's dreams…
If you're not here now you're a "Drunken Boat,"
As Rimbaud's prosodies illuminate the goat:
Illuminati's got you cradle to the grave,
And Baphomet is in the nave…

PART II

East of Eden there's an emerald gate,
That leads the souls of men to shrift,
The path of surfeit leads to the House of Haight;
The Wasteland's miles away to drift…
Playing black jack on a pontoon bridge;
"May the day of my birth perish in the Sun…"
Astounds my grave just like a moonscape on a ridge:
I'm just a paranoid with a gun…

East of Eden there's a cypress tree,
That leads your soul through a conscious stream.
I don't believe in what you cannot see:
"No, I don't want you for a sunbeam…"
My pain is heavier than heaven in the rain,
A living hell inside a schizoid's brain.
No, I don't know what I should spin or chase,
Wasting time in a timeless place…

PART III

East of Eden, a 'New Age' starlet in a dream:
That leads the souls of all these modern story-spinners;
To follow all their sorrows in a summer gleam:
Weary am I, this day, of sinners…
We've been soul mates since the dawn of Tenniel;
A King and Queen immortal: in crimson and in gold.
Yes, your naïveté's a spring perennial:
Let me be young before I'm old…

East of Eden in a dream world 'neath Big Dipper;
That leads the crow's flight, who just scurries on his way;
Where rants the wicked witch in her magic ruby slippers,
Deep in her labyrinths to stray…
Lost in a daydream filled with voodoo arbitrage,
To sell commodities beyond your persiflage,
Where jabberwocky reigns like poppies in the fields;
Just like the curses that she wields…

PART IV

(Let us once more venture, traipsing hand to hand:
And give me my belief in such a Dreamtime land…
Let us once more venture, traipsing hand to hand:
And give me my belief in such a Dreamtime land…
Let us once more venture, traipsing hand to hand:
And give me my belief in such a Dreamtime land…
Let us once more venture, traipsing hand to hand:
And give me my belief in such a Dreamtime land…)

ILLUMINATION 4:20

Seek illumination,
Just a soul that seeks elation,
So lay me down on heaven's ether skies.
Falling is for fallers,
Just a zeitgeist in the alders,
You'll always fall if you don't trust my lies.

Remember to remember,
Just a dead rose in December,
No palm-to-palm concord for the brain dead.
We've founded New Atlantis,
Just a land where plebs are helpless,
To lead you down the roads that you've misled.

Don't count your blessings 'neath a Novocain sky,
If your insight's in the outlook you will never die,
Don't count your blessings 'neath a Novocain sky,
If your insight's in the outlook you will never die…

Seek illumination,
Just a ghost lost in translation,
Mistakes to be mistaken as mistakes;
Your wisdom's got no "secrets,"
Just a precinct full of egrets,
It only seeks to give you what it takes.

You've reached the seventh stratum,
Just a rapture in a spectrum,
It looks like my reflection's in the brine;
The cosmos and your psyche,
Just a perfect synchronicity,
Is melding Jachin-Boaz to your spine.

Don't count your blessings 'neath a Novocain sky,
If your insight's in the outlook you will never die,
Don't count your blessings 'neath a Novocain sky,
If your insight's in the outlook you will never die…

Seek illumination,
Just a walking contradiction,

Forget what you've forgotten to forget.
It's the Age of Aquarius,
Big Brother's now victorious,
A beatnik's just as good as you can get.

The neon lights are pretty,
A broken scene in New York City,
Got a zodiac conjunction in my mind,
I see it in my hindsight,
Just a starlet in the twilight,
A brotherhood of man for all mankind…

Don't count your blessings 'neath a Novocain sky,
If your insight's in the outlook you will never die.
No, don't count your blessings 'neath a Novocain sky…
If your insight's in the outlook you will never die.
If your insight's in the outlook you will never die.
If your insight's in the outlook you will never die.
If your insight's in the outlook you will never die.

DEAR PIANOMAN

Was it you who told me love
should begin with a kiss?
Was it you who told me love
should fall apart like this?
Was it you who told me the heart of
the piano man was broken?
Was it you who told me
that love should remain unspoken?

I know you love me too,
Just not as dearly as your loneliness…
Or cocaine skies that fall
From worlds I'll never understand…

If my letters begin to bleed again
Or I evade you for your memories, my dear:
these bloodroots fall for love.
If my letters begin to bleed again
Or I evade you for your memories, my dear:
these bloodroots fall for love.

Was it your beauty that passed me by
and made a myth of my grace?
Was it your love that passed me by…
and made Septentrion light my space?
Was it you who broke my alibi
to let me know you're broken?
Was it you who told me
that love should remain unspoken?

I know you love me too,
Just not as dearly as your loneliness…
Or cocaine skies that fall
From worlds I'll never understand…

If my letters begin to bleed again
Or I evade you for your memories, my dear:
these bloodroots fall for love.
If my letters begin to bleed again
Or I evade you for your memories, my dear:

these bloodroots fall for love.

(...bridge...)
If my letters begin to bleed again
Or I evade you for your memories, my dear:
these bloodroots fall for love.
If my letters begin to bleed again
Or I evade you for your memories, my dear:
these bloodroots fall for love.

CATCHER IN THE RYE

The past goes on ahead of time,
And tells you: "Don't forget to rime…"
'Cause with all you see comes everything to light.
I heard you crying out to God,
He said: "Don't forget the laws of Sod…"
You're always trying to find your shadow in the night.

'Cause it feels like such a drug and I'm
A moth in naphthalene,
And I won't believe my mind 'til it reminds me…

Don't you catch me now, Catcher in the Rye,
Just because I'll follow through,
Doesn't mean I'm going where…
The Sun don't shine at all, where we go to die:
It doesn't matter who you are,
Or who you've been, it's who you ought to be…
You ought to be…

I tried my best and did my worst,
And so I ought to be the first
To say there's nothing good or bad, it's what you rue…
No, I'm no good at feeling bad,
I guess I'm caught in my own fad;
I beg my loneliness to leave when I'm with you.

'Cause it feels like such a drug and I'm
A man on Clozapine,
And I won't believe my mind 'til it reminds me…

Don't you catch me now, Catcher in the Rye,
Just because I'll follow through,
Doesn't mean I'm going where…
The Sun don't shine at all, where we go to die:
It doesn't matter where you are,
Or where you've been, it's where you ought to be,
You ought to be… You ought to be…

The prophet lags behind the time,
In a hockshop purchased at a dime,

And so the poor man's retributions fill the skies…
I don't know what to do or say,
Expect that everyone is gay,
It's all apologies to wont your alibis…

'Cause it feels like such a drug and I'm
A moth in naphthalene,
And I won't believe my mind 'til it reminds me…

Don't you catch me now, Catcher in the Rye,
Just because I'll follow through,
Doesn't mean I'm going where…
The Sun don't shine at all, where we go to die:
It doesn't matter where you are,
Or where you've been, it's where you ought to be,
You ought to be… You ought to be…
You ought to be…

SUMMER OF LOVE: 1967*

Judy, forget your mind,
It's 1:00 am, you taste like liquor…
The smell of cigarettes
Surrounds us: we're in uteri,
As love befalls us…

And I can hold my own,
And spill my guts, a rolling stone,
In empty theatres: the Grand Ole Opry, and Carnegie.
As time befalls me…

No, she don't *talk in innuendos,*
Living life on angel's dreams,
Where nothing's what it seems.
She fills my *skies with delta blues eyes,*
Living life on angel dust,
With nothing left to trust…

Judy, forget your mind,
It's 2:00 am, these songs will flicker
Your ghostlike minuets;
Like moonlit thoughts for Gemini,
As love befalls us...

And I can hold my own,
And spill my guts, a rolling stone,
In empty theatres: the Grand Ole Opry, and Carnegie.
As time befalls me…

No, she don't *talk in innuendos,*
Living life on angel's dreams,
Where nothing's what it seems.
She fills my *skies with delta blues eyes,*
Living life on angel dust,
With nothing left to trust…

Judy, forget your mind,
It's 3:00 am, it burns like wicker,
From ash to rosettes;
My lovelorn concords refuse to die,

As love befalls us…

And I can hold my own,
And spill my guts, a rolling stone,
In empty theatres: the Grand Ole Opry, and Carnegie.
As time befalls me…

No, she don't *talk in innuendos,*
Living life on angel's dreams,
Where nothing's what it seems.
She fills my *skies with delta blues eyes,*
Living life on angel dust,
With nothing left to trust…

(The last time we felt this,
We were drunk and crazy,
In 1967, for the Summer of Love…
The last time we felt this,
We were on Haight-Ashbury,
In 1967, for the Summer of Love…)

Judy, forget your mind,
It's 4:00 am, our souls will dicker
These celestial opposites;
Like cosmic twins: Dioscuri,
As love befalls us…

And I can hold my own,
And spill my guts, a rolling stone,
In empty theatres: the Grand Ole Opry, and Carnegie.
As time befalls me…

No, she don't *talk in innuendos,*
Living life on angel's dreams,
Where nothing's what it seems.
She fills my *skies with delta blues eyes,*
Living life on angel dust,
With nothing left to trust…

Judy, forget your mind,
It's 5:00 am, this dream's an ichor,
With ethereal silhouettes;

Like lovers' synergies: we can't descry…
As love befalls us…

And I can hold my own,
And spill my guts, a rolling stone,
In empty theatres: the Grand Ole Opry, and Carnegie.
As time befalls me…

No, she don't *talk in innuendos,*
Living life on angel's dreams,
Where nothing's what it seems.
She fills my *skies with delta blues eyes,*
Living life on angel dust,
With nothing left to trust…

Judy, forget your mind,
It's 6:00 am, hook, line, and sinker
These soulful Ethernets…
Like Castor n' Pollux; you mystify (me),
As love befalls us…

And I can hold my own,
And spill my guts, a rolling stone,
In empty theatres: the Grand Ole Opry, and Carnegie.
As time befalls me…

No, she don't *talk in innuendos,*
Living life on angel's dreams,
Where nothing's what it seems.
She fills my *skies with delta blues eyes,*
Living life on angel dust,
With nothing left to trust…

(The last time we felt this,
We were drunk and crazy,
In 1967, for the Summer of Love…
The last time we felt this,
We were on Haight-Ashbury,
In 1967, for the Summer of Love…)

It's just a serenade…

BUSINESS MONKEY

There she stands in a dirndl skirt, and her scarlet hair,
She's got a mind to disagree…
To dream the spells of a hieratic nightmare;
Ain't nothin' but a fantod for Eurydice.
Helter-skelter, doesn't matter, what you've got to tell her,
She dignifies her grace like Desmond Dekker.

Mellow out, you business monkey,
Mellow out, you business monkey.
The world's not praying at your feet,
The world's not praying at your feet…

There he stands in a Leo suit and a Cosmo grin,
He's got milk and honey to spin.
King of laureates in the halls of Ivy;
He walks on a map of Corpus Christi.
Raggle-taggle, hoity-toity, hurly-burly smiles,
He dignifies his pride with wits and wiles.

Mellow out, you business monkey,
Mellow out, you business monkey.
The world's not praying at your feet,
The world's not praying at your feet…

And in her dreams she's spellbound as the dark looms,
She sees the wicked witch fly on a broom…
Can't prophesy the futures in her tarots:
The One-eyed Merchant's and his argots…

There she stands in white and indigo, lost in Dixieland,
Lost in a dream world under Nan…
No, she can't keep up with her own thoughts…
Sings the blues like a scruple at a rate of knots…
Helter-skelter, doesn't matter, what you've got to tell her.
She dignifies her soul like Desmond Dekker.

Mellow out, you business monkey,
Mellow out, you business monkey.
The world's not praying at your feet,
The world's not praying at your feet…

And now she dreams like Eurydice,
Stuck in a Jungian synchronicity…
So keep on dreaming; flights of fantasy:
It's otherworldly curiosity…

(Mellow out, you business monkey,
Mellow out, you business monkey.
The world's not praying at your feet,
The world's not praying at your feet…
The world's not praying at your feet,
The world's not praying at your feet…)

CITY OF THE DAMNED

I see the city of the damned,
Where simians fly to and fro, with minds unmanned.
I see a witch going round and round,
Ring-around-the-rosy, and we all fall down.
(The Wiccan's got no place to go,
Her daemons tell her to never jut the toe.
Got eigenvalues in my head,
And deus ex machina's here to take my stead.)

Welcome to the city,
The city of the damned . . .
Welcome to the city,
The city of the damned . . .

Martello towers made of emerald,
Where Oz's consorts are now bought and sold.
The hamadryad's dead in the head,
And Gog and Magog seem to've lost their cred.
(Yes, Ockham's razor's splitting hairs;
And ragtag and bobtail cannot keep their heirs.
Orwellian notions in my brain,
And all my thoughts have gone insane to sane.)

Welcome to the city,
The city of the damned . . .
Welcome to the city,
The city of the damned . . .

The witch's Shabbat's in the coven,
Where Masons sleep and dine at Miser's Inn.
Got Stabat Mater in my dreams;
The "Doors of Perception" are never what they seem.
(Got Huxley's shadow at my feet,
There's no one in the "New World" I would rather meet.
I'm just a Leibniz with no soul,
No dolce vita left to face my dole.)

Welcome to the city,
The city of the damned . . .
Welcome to the city,

The city of the damned . . .

A "Brave New World" is in the books,
The Book of books is full of commie crooks.
A superego's Freudian slip,
Is just the soul's hegira from a Moloch crypt.
(I've never seen this place before,
Sarvodaya's ghost is behind the doors.
The Devil's "Golden Dawn" is full;
A stalemate's the only trick he's yet to pull.)

Welcome to the city,
The city of the damned . . .
Welcome to the city,
The city of the damned . . .

Got secret Shaktis on my case,
And Nazi saboteurs've got me on the chase.
I'm being seduced by my seditions;
Throwing Molotovs at the anti-Prussians.
(I'm here to stave the tree of life;
As casus belli's underlying strife,
Reverses "State Fair" to "Fair State."
It's the New World Order: raise them all to bate.)

Welcome to the city,
The city of the damned . . .
Welcome to the city,
The city of the damned . . .

I've got an evil on my mind,
And if I share it it's no longer mine.
Don't let the cat out of the bag;
Failed to differentiate what's begun to lag.
(I've got a despot in my head,
And his suicide machines: better dead than Red.
I'm just a sultan with no sails,
A "Prince of Peace" who cannot 'scape his ails.)

Welcome to the city,
The city of the damned . . . (x 2)

STAIRWAY TO HELL

You found the "House of the Rising Sun,"
With seditious eyes and a loaded gun,
Thinking: "This is what the world has me to dun…"
It's Iscariot's kiss on the Son of Man
With a flintlock gun: a flash in the pan;
You sold your soul for something Black and Tan.

Can't catch your breath if you're not running out of air,
Can't change the things you see if your dreams don't dare to dare;
The midnight gavel spreads its thunder through the sky…

I've got the Devil on my heels again,
I've got the Devil on my heels…
I've got the Devil on my heels again,
I've got the Devil on my heels…
And he's trying to drag me down,
Yeah, he's trying to drag me down…

The witch and all her eidolons
Are here to stay and then they're gone,
Incorporate the firms to all her pawns…
The Dakota's now a haunted place,
Where the spirits try to distill your grace,
"The Catcher in the Rye" was on your case…

The sound of flies was like electric storms,
Flying monkeys clad in soldiers' uniforms,
The midnight gavel spreads its thunder through the sky…

I've got the Devil on my heels again,
I've got the Devil on my heels…
I've got the Devil on my heels again,
I've got the Devil on my heels…
And he's trying to drag me down,
Yeah, he's trying to drag me down…

When Mephisto came to talk to you,
Rebel angel spiels without a clue,
Said: "This is what the world has done to you."
And he showed you signs of World War III,

In a field of dust in Galilee,
Said: "This is how the world will fall to me."

Your Wilhelm ghost still puts your conscience on a whim,
And black light humour turns the world from bright to dim,
The midnight gavel spreads its thunder through the sky…

I've got the Devil on my heels again,
I've got the Devil on my heels…
I've got the Devil on my heels again,
I've got the Devil on my heels…
And he's trying to drag me down,
Yeah, he's trying to drag me down…

O Satan, my Satan, thou art but a dunce,
Every harlot was a virgin once.
And your sins cannot know the garb from the man,
Nor can you change Kate into Nan.
We're in Tinttenhurst and we're lost 'neath a sundog,
"No, this is not here" in the fog…

Shadows of doubt on the walls I've misread,
Must go down all the roads I've misled.
If perdition is real but your freedoms are not,
Tell me why did you seek what you sought?
Listen to me backward, and I'll tell you of an afterword
O Morning Star, surround me like a gird…

FASCIST RADIO NWO

Ingsoc's in the mindless ears,
And I don't know where I am, I'm not all here:
It's a Ram Dass inner-fear.
Standing by the Lord of the Flies,
The Leo stares into a monarch full of lies;
Divine truth never dies.

Here's "Mein Kampf" on a dusty sill,
Watch a film noir 'bout the "Triumph of the Will,"
Your jewels and your pills.
The conquistador on a purple horse,
Who just conquers lands in Emerald under Mors;
It's an ego trip's recourse.

But I can't escape what the past has done to me,
And I can't foresee what the future's wont to see,
Don't listen to the fascist radio…

Relativity's in the rain,
It's like static in the figments of my pain,
Where the tin god must refrain.
The Gestapo's got an eye
On Freemasons and on angels in the sky,
Fie this fiefdom, fie!

See the isomorphic freak,
Who just prances like a Gestalt among the meek:
"If you think what you won't speak."
The scarecrow don't know what's behind…
But he knows there's nothing real except the mind:
"If you seek what you won't find."

But I can't escape what the past has done to me,
And I can't foresee what the future's wont to see,
Don't listen to the fascist radio…

Talking to myself in flow,
Tell me something that I don't already know;
Like dead angels in the snow.
Dorothy Dixers must abode,

When she bides her time like a star without a lode,
Her mind is now corrode.

See Lolita's ecclesia,
As she prays for ecce homo amnesia,
Or a moshav messiah.
Hear the fascist radio,
Hear a Hitler speech that condescends the low,
With things they ought to know.

But I can't escape what the past has done to me,
And I can't foresee what the future's wont to see,
Don't listen to the fascist radio…

The man inside the radio,
Just diffuses rimes from times we'll never know;
Got nowhere else to go…
All my presumptions die for love,
When I listen to your songs: our souls to Jove;
Where feelings push and shove…

Give your chattels to the thief,
Selling wars that just lobotomize our grief,
Just to turn another leaf...
We're just spirits full of fear;
All our meanings dissipate to something clear,
To something we can't hear…

But I can't escape what the past has done to me,
And I can't foresee what the future's wont to see,
Don't listen to the fascist radio…

You deaden love like cyanide,
You would take your life for all the things you hide;
But it's time to turn the tide…
Don't deny what you love most,
Just to lose yourself and meander as a ghost;
To observe the Lord of Hosts…

A robin red breast in a cage,
Hellish proverbs that refuse to turn the page;
All heaven's in a rage…

You're just happy 'cause you're free,
To condemn your thoughts, like daemons in a dree;
To see what they can't see…

But I can't escape what the past has done to me,
And I can't foresee what the future's wont to see,
Don't listen to the fascist radio…

Don't let your candelabras die,
In a hopeless room, to propagate your lies,
'gainst what failure vies…
No, I may never find my path,
To the moment time got lost in the aftermath;
Like a phoenix in a bath…

Forget what you've come to forget,
Yes, you raffled out your odds and paid the debt;
And it all leads to regret…
It's M-K Ultra mind control:
No one sees the truth, you cannot teach the soul:
When heaven takes a stroll…

But I can't escape what the past has done to me,
And I can't foresee what the future's wont to see,
Don't listen to the fascist radio…

If you ever wonder where you are,
When preachers preach and fast for caviar,
Your power's like a czar…
We're nothing more than troubadours,
But these corollaries won't open up the doors,
To haunt the corridors...

No, you're not 'who you think you are,'
Just like a lonely shimmer: or corollas in the tar;
Your soul to burn and char…
Profess the kismets that you choose:
You'd rather be yourself in someone else's shoes;
You've got nothing left to lose.

But I can't escape what the past has done to me,
And I can't foresee what the future's wont to see,

Don't listen to the fascist radio…

It's like a blind man's imago,
Keep turning off your senses like a radio;
Or a fascist on the go…
Seems to privatize our fears,
To overwhelm our wisdoms drowning in the mere,
Don't pretend that you can't hear…

It's like a prism in the light:
Your true colors always seem to lose their sight;
In the rain man's holy rite.
And now you're blinded by deceit:
As you swathe yourself in someone else's sheets,
Your brainstorms turn to sleet.

But I can't escape what the past has done to me,
And I can't foresee what the future's wont to see,
Don't listen to the fascist radio…

You lost your mind in Xanadu,
Trying to find a place to meet your Waterloo;
But you lost your point of view…
Tried to feel the words you said…
But Nirvana's hard to find amongst the dead;
And so you lost your soul instead…

My thoughts keep running off the hills,
What's pre-written never falls beyond its thrills;
Just don't listen to these shills…
'Cause when I saw the roads ahead;
I felt the night just twisting concepts in my head:
To mislead what I've misled.

But I can't escape what the past has done to me,
And I can't foresee what the future's wont to see,
Don't listen to the fascist radio…

The prince of sutra won't pretend,
That his paradox won't breach what it should mend;
Or what it should portend…
He puts you in a time machine,

Back to time spans lacking space; you've never seen…
The places that you've been.

Nothing proves my pain is real,
I guess I lost my mind to forget what I can feel;
With my scruples reel-to-reel…
All my daydreams fall behind;
Where the 'Gates of Eden' opened up my mind;
To make my thoughts go blind…

But I can't escape what the past has done to me,
And I can't foresee what the future's wont to see,
Don't listen to the fascist radio…

Your pride must slake your zodiac eyes,
To see meaning where confusion drowns the skies;
You're full of fibs and lies…
Our sense of time must give us pause;
To stifle gods with such lacunas in the cause,
Like the mystic's inner-pause…

Yes, the clairvoyant cannot speak;
The future's burning leaves of absence near a creek:
"To find what you won't seek…"
Your fear's ahead of you at times,
Like a boatman in a desert, cask and chimes;
It gets lost from time to time.

But I can't escape what the past has done to me,
And I can't foresee what the future's wont to see,
Don't listen to the fascist radio…

Backward thoughts relive the past,
Replace my instinct with a whim that cannot last;
Don't nail your colors to the mast.
It seems divergent to my wills,
Nothing seems as real to me as nature's frills;
For Phoenicians on the Hill…

All my memories haunt the gloom,
They remember each complaint that hits the loom;
And I'm left speechless in my room…

My conscience leads a double life,
Nothing comes my way unless it spares my strife;
When nothing seems so rife.

But I can't escape what the past has done to me,
And I can't foresee what the future's wont to see,
Don't listen to the fascist radio…

A dulcet tender as the ears;
Angels dancing in a disco with their fears;
Like a slight within their smears…
A moment trembling at its height,
Lest I forebode myself to no one in my rites;
Like a lonely bird in flight…

Poetic swimmers, encroaching tides,
Sometimes the mystery's more intriguing when it hides;
I'm lost on the other side…
Your ghost is in the wrong machine,
Asking questions that refuse to flee the scene;
No, you'll never spill the beans…

But I can't escape what the past has done to me,
And I can't foresee what the future's wont to see,
Don't listen to the fascist radio…

If you don't live the full extent,
You'll be wistful when you've got to pay the rent,
To hide the meanings that you meant…
Explore the mysteries that you wane,
Explaining God away whenever you feel vain:
Like a mystery in the rain…

So cast your scruples to the throes;
If you're a sinner you should reap the sins you sow;
But you shouldn't stoop so low…
Yes, quantum poets in their reign,
Perjuries never fly when half the mind's insane,
Like a schism in the brain.

But I can't escape what the past has done to me,
And I can't foresee what the future's wont to see,

Don't listen to the fascist radio…

Your questions don't create beliefs,
But your mind creates your thoughts, like burning leafs;
Yet your psyche's in the reefs…
I hope you never lose your stead;
When tomorrow's gone, you'll be thankful when you're dead;
The light is in your head.

Dictums drowning in the sea,
I just can't understand what's happening to me;
To invoke the doubts I'll free…
You hide your thoughts from everyone,
As you repeat yourself and all the things you've done;
With your conscience on the run…

But I can't escape what the past has done to me,
And I can't foresee what the future's wont to see,
Don't listen to the fascist radio…

Ever since your odysseys,
I sang Anchises' songs when all my twinges seize;
The notion hell must freeze.
Seems none of my ideals have ears,
Yes, I fear my own beliefs, believe my fears;
The past is in arrears...

There's a sibyl down the road,
Who predicts the road will end with Ranvier's node,
So don't leave behind your ode...
"The Catcher in the Rye" will fall,
Yet we fear the pain of a burning voodoo doll:
Illumination lights us all…

But I can't escape what the past has done to me,
And I can't foresee what the future's wont to see,
Don't listen to the fascist radio…

No, I can't escape what the past has done to me,
And I can't foresee what the future's wont to see,
Don't listen to the fascist radio…
Don't listen to the fascist radio…

In the beginning was the nothingness of life. I was
a hermetic chapman, an anchorite, a nomad in
God's somatic dream; a thief in search of
something mysterious, which becomes a sort of
self-mirage. Disabled by the fear of being
disabled, I walked on the pathless path like an
empty-minded lazar, from here to there but finding
nothing in between. "Meaningless, meaningless,
everything is meaningless," says the Teacher. But
his meaninglessness was never meant to be. My
thoughts were like tyros trying to act out the parts
of a complexity they couldn't understand; and so
my paradox kept changing like a transient
dimension. In states of hypomania, my spirit was
made purblind by the incubus that embodies Dead
Sea politicians, deriding the dust in each other's
pathways; though dust is always the same no
matter how you look at it. The two voices in my
head were like Paleozoic philosophers, arguing
about the texture of the light, the depth of the well,
the existence of God. I became comfortably numb
within myself, like a fly in a caste of amberoid; I
couldn't even sense the coming of the spider. My
mind became the only place for conversation,
describing itself to the secret silence of its own
enigma, like a self-conscious mirror in search of
its true reflection, but finding it nowhere, seeing
nothing except the nothingness within itself. Life
became nothing more than a forgetful memory...
and it suborned me to peek into my mind like an
unknowable messenger, and find that the stairway,
not its descent, was what I feared the most; merely
the possibility of the descent, into the darkest
depth, into the realm of absolute oblivion, no
longer aware of Syrian sweatshops, or Al Capone
presidencies, each of them treading each other's
heels like demigod hell-bounds, to accomplish the
abomination that leads to desolation. "Are you not
mindful of your own mind?" saith the spirit of a
man. And from his carbon mist I heard de Molay's

ghost decry: "What is it this world has forgotten
that the Son of Man himself cannot find refuge in
the churches built upon His name?" Ay, life to me
was a faux-naif mime, who performed my likes
and dislikes whether I liked it or not. But however
severe the malaises of the collective mind, I
traveled on, wearied by the imagoes of God, yet
entranced by the ideal of some noetic Otherworld;
not quite nolens volens, but somewhere in
between each notion, willing to speak but
unwilling to be heard. Life incurred a literature I
condemned within myself to understand the very
depths of hell; meanwhile, Heaven hovered
somewhere above my knowledge, like God's noli
me tangere, awaiting His re-birth in nature's
ovum. Dyslexic to God, I dug a labyrinth within
myself to elude His eye, even though there was
nothing to fear; the incubus only existed insofar as
I was willing to hide. But a man lost in the
melodrama of his own fantasies, fears himself like
a self-conscious ghost in a samizdat fire,
replicating the dreams of a no-hoper before the
many mirrors of a fear. The man on the podium is
as insightful as his outlook, and he repeats himself
as carefully as a geometric satrap near a map,
basking in the capriccio of publicans and
Pharisees, handing out invisible pamphlets printed
by Morgan le Fay's scepter to the unsuspecting
proletarians of mass and distribution, to spread an
eclipse that would blind the hungry and hunger the
blind. But God's eye kept watch over the
dwindling golden road and before the haunted
forest He openly declared: BEWARE THE ONE-
EYED MERCHANT!!! His consciousness is more
invective to native silences than the throes and
nightmares of a prelapsarian shaman, who
secludes the talking ghosts of the past to a velvet
room where music cannot possibly be sound. "If
you tap upon an empty jar," saith he, "the
emptiness mourns the echo of existence." He
differs with a difference, and teaches blindness
never to settle for its groping. The man's mirage

expends our convictions by force-feeding us false
hope: Pontius Politics! Ay, the mind becomes a
self-enraptured circus, a highbrow chimp being
brainwashed at a Chaplin flick! Moloch! Moloch!
The Keeper's in the Clock! And the Wicked Witch
of the Western World knows the Pontiff like the
husband she defrocks! God's light to me
questioned my pain like an unsatisfied mystery,
despising my conscience like some Blind Freddie,
in a selfsame prison where over-informed citizens
talk about politics for the rest of their knowable
lives. Each day my happiness suffered like a
burning vesture, and each day I added to the fires
of its riots, white as a blind man' blitzkrieg, like
some absurd Gotterdammerung domed by
germanium witches, whose spell assumed it would
never be broken, nor unspoken, awaiting some
pre-estrus political god who proofreads his
propaganda to the living relics of his lost disciples:
"The instruments of peace are necessary to
preserve the war… The instruments of peace are
necessary to preserve the war." Like one who,
weary of the night yet dreams himself within it,
and sets his moorings so deeply into the grounds
of his deceit that no truth ever escapes him, the
man is a prisoner in a rogue's gallery, a shirker of
shame, unwilling to damn his soul but acting upon
the dearth like a sick little peasant child, a
mischievous recreant entranced with the spirit of
fear, with the speech of agnostic angels, inciting
the clouds to rain upon the neediest seeds of his
dementia. Like an arrant armyworm's navigation
through unsettled fields of dust, his sapience, like
a dying old man at a bugaboo rally, fills his pate
with the knowledge of a dead man, yet, like a
trapeze artist on a tightrope set afire, he concedes
his victuals to be wary of any loss that wages itself
against the "memoirs of his struggle," to be as
exact in guilt as a portion of lust weighed against
the desires of a lecher. And so the Oligarch's
magic spell led astray the dying, like
Machiavellian monks in black-light monasteries,

with a yellowed Timbuktu map and a grey zone
compass, that the living might never know what is
to become of them until they die. But verily I say:
"In the tribunals of left versus right, the only way
out is up." For a man and his disaster, himself
oblivious of his mien, goes to his grave
unfathomed of the deed that damns him. It's the
everlasting idleness of a man in the everlasting
desert of himself, to become a heptahedral augur
made spendthrift by doubt, by fear, by a
Revelation that the Anointed Ones must never
dare to speak: We will no longer die for Caligula,
nor wield to the endless charades and bargains of
the One-eyed Merchant, nor wend down godless
paths that chase felicities to their graves, nor give
our grief to Devils, then inquire them like old
institutions of truth, nor reckon with every fire that
threatens the House of Balaam, nor misconstrue
the diaphanous faces of Zion as the elders of
Barabbas, nor misguide the grace of prophets
through the idioms of Baal, nor inveigle peace like
an old mistress that we'd never dare to love or
understand, nor incite ourselves to outrage beyond
the circumstance of our own mores, nor converse
of pointless errands that vainly try to originate
from the Unknown, and return with no knowledge
of the life that never ceases to inquire the Abyss
where no life enters. "Let the dead
bury their own dead!"

(…9,260 words…)

***

Meanwhile, I started writing again and completely revised my
play: "Ur-AMLETHUS."

So far I had only written a very small part of what I had in
mind. I wanted my novel to eventually be of Trollopian proportions,
at least a thousand pages---a kind of Metamodernist wonderland for
the literati… to call a halt on my own experience with mental illness
and creativity.

As crazy as that sounds… in my mind the word impossible

doesn't exist, and that's where the possibilities begin.

My story is personified by my own ambitions as a writer, but it could be yours if you don't listen to my stipulations about thc Ncw World Order: always be mindful of the Government or the Government will be mindful of you…

I felt so strongly about my purpose, my mission, that I printed a few copies my early novel, and prepared them for specific destinations, with my fingerprint, in black ink, on the cover page of each manuscript. I left them anonymously in three places in New York City: the Public Library, the University Library, and a small bookstore in Greenwich Village, like some sort of dissident in a lawless paragon.

I felt such a tremendous sense of purpose that I truly believed my novel would meet its fate no matter what. It was my Zeitgeist! Crazy or not, I was on a mission…. almost as if I had been chosen by God ever since I was a child…

It was at this time that the ringing in my ears started…

I read somewhere that the ancient Greeks thought that if you had a ringing in the ears, it was God trying to transmit His knowledge into your brain with extrasensory epiphanies and modalities…

Could that possibly be true? Was that where I was getting all my knowledge about the Universe, my music and my book? Was it a gift from God…? Had I been chosen…?

The crazy thing is… I even had three different psychics tell me that I was going to become a professional singer-songwriter and novelist, and that I was going in to travel across North America with my book and my CD, which had always been a dream of mine. I wanted to put a mattress in the back of a Volkswagen van and travel to big cities and small towns, from bookstore to bookstore…

They even said that I would be on television and on the radio, promoting my book and my music.

I remember, before I left the first psychic's house, she said to me: "Don't give up on your music! Don't give up…"

***

Meanwhile, I started getting the urge to toke up again. I wanted to do nothing other than get high and finish writing my novel. I was exploring all the possibilities---like weans in my scruples.

When I got to my room, however, I felt so exhausted from my constant fretting and absurd plans that I threw myself on my bed and started bawling: an amorist alone in a grot…

Madness to me is like an odalisque armoire in the fires of despair---the Anthropomorphic Cabinet: a Freudian stench. "A kind of allegory destined to illustrate a certain forbearance, to scent out the countless narcissistic smells that waft out of all our drawers."

I couldn't even walk on an overpass without imagining myself jumping into the arterial thruway below, or a bridge into the gully. I couldn't stop thinking about suicide. It was like a cassette tape in some kind of Dalek-like henotheism.

For about an hour at the University that day, I sat by the library window and imagined myself leaping to my death over and over and over again. Then I would try to concentrate on the dissertation I had to write for my Ulysses class, but I would just revert to my suicidal thoughts like some kind of windowless reprise. And at night, I would feel so empty that I cried into my pillow, frustrated with everything: my lack of sleep, my suicidal urges, my deep desire to do drugs again, my constant sense of worthlessness and failure, my intolerable megalomania.

***

When I finally showed my poetry to Harold Bloom, the berg Professor of Humanities at New York University, he said: "Maybe you can invent your own genre, your own genus, like James Joyce… Remember, the future of genius is always metaphorical…"

***

Then, one day, I saw something on television that made me very suspicious as to why I felt this way day in and day out. It intrigued me so much that I decided to look it up for myself. I went to a website that would tell me everything I needed to know. What I would go on to read would devastate me:

Bipolar Disorder: a mental disease characterized by episodes of mania, hypomania and uncontrollable stages of euphoria and depression. The disorder is common in highly creative people though the reason for this is still unknown. Sufferers of the disease go through a refrain of specific symptoms such as sleeplessness, self-loathing, unrealistic or delusional ideas and goals, i.e. a self-motivated belief about a special mission or being the 'chosen one' for something, suicidal ideation, and exhaustion…

As soon as I finished reading this, I felt as if my heart had suddenly been clasped by an invisible graft, like a popper that furnished my isolation, with nothing but highbrow insolence and cheap impertinence to justify my stint: cheek by jowl. I went to my room and sat down on my bed, rocking back and forth, holding my head. "Oh God... something's wrong with me. I'm crazy... I'm fucking crazy…"

Then I suddenly stopped crying and became extremely angry, seething at my indabas. I kept looking for someone to blame: those bastards at school, who had reduced my self-esteem to a perennial travesty… now that I was completely maniacal toward my own derision toward the world, like Chris McCandless…

Maybe it was genetic… or perhaps I had done it to myself with my own hyperactive thought-process, which, by the way, is yet another symptom. That's why a lot of writers are bipolar: they think too much, they over-think everything. Also, it has been shown that students who had straight A's at school are four times more likely to become bipolar in their early twenties than the average person.

Maybe I was powerless over my own personal shunts, and the electronic bypasses of my brain, to jolt my prerogatives with winter fire, like a sarong in oil set alight. Or maybe I needed help from a psychiatrist. Nevertheless, everything seemed like a goddamn catch-22 to me. I wanted to destroy everything I owned. I wanted to erase my identity, my memory—the navigations of a spotless mind on untroubled waters. I wanted throw my book into the trash and just give up.

Writing a book like this was absurd… impossible!

CHAPTER EIGHT

It was around this time that I really started to lose my grasp on reality. I was extremely paranoid and exceedingly chary in my rites of passage as an artist, sparing my own indulgence. It was like an anchorage in a refuge of personal motives, by whose perfidy I abided my constancy as a recluse and as a writer... it was like a leitmotif in a catalogue of dead memories.

People could hear my thoughts: my internal denunciations, whether good or bad.

They were afraid of me---and I didn't know why...

And within my acrimony grew, like an ephemeral foetus, and my eccentricities became more and more theatrical, like some sort of gonzo in the conurbations of the art world: the urban sprawl of Greenwich Village. But their persecution of my ways became more pungent than they could introvert for themselves. It's in vogue to be egotistical these days.

It seems everyone is unique except for me...

In the olden days, if you wanted to be famous, you had to be a genius of some sort...

Now, anyone can be famous, because the Freemasons pull on all the subliminal yarns of culture, like masters of illusion.

People like stupid shit... but not me. I'm wildly divergent. I wanted to write a book and music for intelligent people: intellectuals, poets, artists, bohemians, professors, and students of literature... It's a small but dedicated audience, dyed-in-the-wool, and Greenwich Village was full of them.

I was like Poldy in Soho...

You see, I'm very introverted, very strange, and at times socially taciturn, and some might say that this is exactly my problem: that I believe in my own illness---I've characterized it to my very character. It circumvents my pride to be still as a nightspot to interrogate, complicating corridors for nothing but a spell of omniscience.

Ah, you see...? It's always unexpected. I never know when everything I believe is real will transform into something else altogether, like a gorgon. I never know when the subconscious arachnid approaches me for its daily subversion of my conscience. One moment I am euphoric, the other... almost suicidal, looking for the end within myself, but never quite reaching the point of no reprieve. There's an imbalance of dopamine in me that I can't describe, nor portray to the arterial modems of my soul, even as it lights up my diaphanous annex in the sight of God, which I can only presume is the hereafter on the winding stairways of creativity...

I think bipolar is a bit of a prejudice, jaunting my will to become it---an anode in the negative electrodes of my mind: the junctures of my own official pitons, with which I shall ascend to the heavens, like a paschal for ingrates. And so I decided I would begin to write about it, to expunge myself of its presence, to exhume myself of its rites, like an exorcism in the dioramas of Nairobi, where solitude reigns heavy on the soul, like some kind of preterit madness in the laments of sainthood...

I did it to evoke a feeling. I wanted you to feel what I feel every moment of the day---uncertainty. Am I crazy, or am I simply more sensible to the truth? It was like a pyretic presentiment in the middling, like a pluvial anecdote with a dry sense of humour, which yet parches wisdom like a node, whose will we desiccate. Whatever the truth, I could not bode either reprisal without feigning my own gothic insentience, where even truth neglects its own dotage---it overflows the measure of light.

Do you see how my mind works now? It never stops flattering itself with its own bugaku---it toadies its own absolution, like a Creole in New Orleans, drinking bourbon for the sake of his adenine, which is in us all, like endocrine in the blood of an archangel. And this is what sent me on my expedition after all. I wanted to figure it out---all of it. So, as others had done, I began to write down my thoughts---an avaricious and acquisitive kind of prose that subdued me like an ormer. And what would come out would be so strange as to make me repulse at my own idiolect. But even as it repulsed me, it lured me in even more deeply, like a liar in a boat who keeps sinking as long as he keeps lying, though he cannot help himself to stoke his own dishonesty---even as it emotes his sensibility to disappear. The choice is yours, even though it wears you out to think about it---like a polystyrene despotism.

What came out of my stipulation, for whatever reason, appeared to me like a play appears to the playwright who wrote it: familiar though differently staged than in his own mind. I'll warn you, it's an abominable pleasure---impossible to resist.

I just don't buy it unless it's true… however sumptuous in the spirit to fathom its impedance, which could never swivel my mind to such a self-befuddlement, and which bewilders the omens of my mead like a turnstile---a revolving barrier to ensue the reversal of the gist within the acrogens of my dross…

But soon, very soon, the Government would find an ingress into my mind. They could read my thoughts. Ever since the ringing in my ears had begun, various people around me could read my thoughts telepathically. Everywhere I went, people would threaten me, while others would push me forward, a few people even spit on me… and sometimes, they even bleated at me like a lamb.

You see, the Nazis didn't lose the war. They were still trying to win it: with MK-Ultra mind control… as they had done with Hitler, who also had a ringing in the ears.

***

It only takes a moment…

I was alone in my room at Hotel Chelsea, and I was holding the gun against my right temple. I had thought about it hundreds of times over the years---it was part of my diurnal frame of mind, a repetitive torrent of thoughts that seemed beyond my hegemony to overthrow the subjugation of madness, yet somehow part of my inner-guise. It was my id… I had never intended my life to take the jaunt it had taken, and yet, it was absurd to think that I'd had no choice over the matter. Surely I was free to think for myself, but nevertheless, I felt as if I had chosen to be choiceless: I was mad.

The ringing in my ears…

My life had been a dire struggle---a dismal fringe around my spirit, adjunct as a transmitter of wisdom for reprobates: a satellite in the mind of Apollo. But at least it had been under control before my ears had begun to ring. It sounded like a computer frequency going through my brain. It had literally driven me insane.

I was insane now, but, it wasn't my fault...

They, the Government, had complete control over me with their supercomputer. I was being brainwashed, and sometimes, they would send me messages and induce me with specific dreams. Yes, they... that's all I could call them, simply because I did not know what else to call them. I didn't even know who "they" were. But who other than the Government would be so sophisticated as to implant me with a microchip in my left wrist? It even had corners and edges when I fiddled around with it...

Indeed, I was being brainwashed by some kind of unknown cogency, an empyreal dacoit of post world Nazism---the so-called Aryans, whose emanation was now inculcated into my brain, like a Polack's presentiments about the war for your mind: Prison Planet.

I thought for sure I was being followed by a satellite...

The city was like a modern prolepsis against the human spirit, wherein you could not tell that it was so unless you had the intellect to see it. It was something that, for whatever reason, no one could even talk about without a dreadful fear taking over their entire nervous system, like shell shock in Nam---a nexus of terror and trepidation.

The people around me were afraid of something...

Whatever it was, it must surely be the Government. Either way, I was in a terminal situation, not because of the gun which I held against my right temple, but because of the external world, which I still did not know for sure actually existed.

***

The problem was that I could no longer tell the difference between what was real, and what I had intended into the world myself. I remember one time... I was walking to Barnes and Noble, and I saw a truck. On the side of the truck, it said: THE SHOW MUST GO ON... When I got to Barnes and Noble, I grabbed a random book and read the following sentence: "Did he not read what was written on the side of that truck?"

It was an external world which I now understood completely. I understood how the Universe worked, and yet I knew nothing of my own mind. It was a paradox, like Heisenberg's uncertainty principle for betokens---omens of ecstasy and melancholy, all at once twined with the shadow of doubt: I clearly misread the writing on the wall... more than once.

How had I gotten to this point? I didn't know, but I understood the possibilities. And each possibility had its own way of torturing me from a distance, like a detached lullaby for my own deviances, to dissociate from the truth and have a parlance within myself...

The first possibility was the one I hated the least: I was insane. I hated this possibility the least because it involved no one else but me. If I was insane, I could dismiss everything that had happened to me as falderal and nothing more. The second possibility was slightly worse: I was being brainwashed into becoming a cosmic Antichrist with each new message, returning one last time to wreak havoc on humanity in Hitler's Postmodern guise---a gambit in the politics of Aquarius. The third possibility was that I was the reincarnation of Christ, with scourge marks on my back and my right side pierced, come to bring Salvation to the world from an unparalleled and invisible gubernatorial evil. What I hated the most was that, no matter which possibility I had inherited, each had its own abhorrent attributes...

All of them bore the temptation to pull the trigger.

***

It only takes a moment...

For the time being, the "moment" was only in my mind, but I knew that it would come, sooner or later. I had a choice to make, and yet, what kind of choice could I possibly make considering the circumstance? My anger toward the world had steadily grown into a savage discordance that I could no longer bear, not only because of everything I had endured to get to this point, but also because my fate was beyond my control, it was written by the felt tips of an ancient prophesy---like "The Satanic Verses."

And yet, I was miserable, because I was all-knowing in a world where being all-knowing is not to your advantage, because the people around me seemed... almost obtuse to their own realities. It was as if something had gone wrong with their genetics. And so, as a result of this depravity and social decadence, I was always alone...

I didn't know whether to question God or to persist with His will, like a burning ester in my heart...

But there was still hope... there was always hope, because I knew I wasn't insane. These things had happened to me... they had not been imaginary. It wasn't just a figment of my imagination: my own eidetic grail, which is to be filled with the blood of angels--- Armageddon. All of it had been real, and the future was also real though not yet perfunctory, or so it seemed to me at the time. Was my destiny prewritten in the stars...?

How could I tell? After all, the neo-Nazis of Congress had put a microchip in my left wrist. There was no way of telling just how much control they had over my mind, save without the flames of ire to attract sensibility.

How could I tell which thoughts were mine, and which thoughts were theirs...?

'This is our Zeitgeist!'

Yes, I had received the messages, and then seen various people around me looking at me as if I was the grim reaper, in the guise of a cosmic Christ, and confirming that I had received it by evaluating my reaction---like a veneer on my affectations, a viscose in a rayon, which I cannot endow without giving dories to my disciples, to fish for truth in the Acheron, which yet cannot try the cause.

***

Yes, they had seen the horror on my face when I had been walking home from Calvin's apartment. The message had been loud and clear, like a loach in my tassel---that if I did not do the will of the Government, I was on my way to destroying the world by opening the seven seals, and thus unleashing the horrors of the Apocalypse on all humanity---a worldwide scourge…

I had covered my mouth with my hand and looked at the woman in the car to my left. She looked at me fearfully, with a dreadful confirmation: I had seen the various exchanges of acknowledgment between the so-called plebs. There was no escape. I still can't describe what I saw that day. It was like the wrath of God---fire falling from the sky.

I looked to my left with tears in my eyes, and the woman in the car said: "Yep… he got the message."

When I got to my room, I immediately picked up my Bible for answers…

I turned the pages to the "Book of Revelation" and read the following passage:

"And he performed great and miraculous signs, even causing fire to come down from heaven to earth in full view of men. Because of the signs he given power on behalf of the first beast, he deceived the inhabitants of the earth."

I thought I had understood the message. The first beast was Hitler, and I was inadvertently following in his footsteps…

This passage was about the Antichrist.

What's happening to me…?

I knew that people could read my thoughts, because they would sometimes reply to them, or react to them, like nodes of disparity. Everyone in town knew exactly who I was. Some called me the Egyptian, others bleated at me like a lamb, others openly insulted me, some accused me of working for INGSOC, others looked at me as if I were a cosmic Christ, saying: "That's Him… That's Jesus!"

It had happened several times. But I ignored it... I didn't want it to be true.

I remember once, when I entered the bus in front of the hospital, a young man had been sitting to the right with his girlfriend. He looked at me and then he whispered to his girlfriend: "That's Jesus."

It was as if it had been embedded in my DNA from birth. I thought it was the genesis of my ego, the exodus of my subconscious id and nothing more... before the Order of Palladium becomes intrinsic to my personal truth.

"Who's your partner in crime?" the lady asked the cashier, spitefully looking at me like a criminal. And the cashier, with a horrible expression on her face, looked at me and replied: "ING-SOC." I knew exactly what that meant. It meant English Socialism. She had taken the expression directly from George Orwell's "1984," which caused me great distress because that was the year I had been born. What was worse was that I had never opted to be a part of the revolution.

One night, I sat in front of my television, and I began to change the channels… I got to the Shopping Network. They all casually kept marketing their product. Then one of them said: "I'm just going to cough now… REVOLUTION!"

There was a camera in my television!!!

***

I had never given anyone the permission to put a microchip in my left wrist. This is what incensed me the most. It had all been done without my knowledge.

The microchip had been implanted without my consent…

Years later, the "cyst" had been activated at a convenient time, while I was listening to music in my room, with headphones on, so that I would initially believe that I had damaged my hearing. But it was eventually revealed to me that it was not ear damage… my hearing was intact. And so now I was in the process of betraying a cause I had never asked to be a part of… No matter what I did, the world would condemn me, they would accuse me of crimes I did not commit, they would crucify me, only in a twenty-first century context ---an assent for the biomes of my spirit.

And so I incessantly browsed through "1984," to find other

instances in which I could confirm my sanity. And everyday I re-called the one moment that would forever debilitate my will to live.

On that night I had been walking home when suddenly, this thought entered my brain:

<u>IAM=AMI</u>
FOREVER

The thought itself would've been innocent enough, but as soon as it entered my brain... her presence had literally taken over my body like a spectre of chills, from head to toe, and I knew that it was her. It started in my brain and swooshed all the way down to my feet in an instant. The feeling was so overwhelming that I almost fell to my knees on the sidewalk. It was as if her ghost had taken possession of me for that brief moment, and we had shared the same presence in one body. It felt as if God had touched me on top of the head, and revealed to me that she was my soul mate---she was my celestial twin.

"Each has his twin; not one of them is alone..."

When I got to my room a few minutes after the occurrence, I sat down and cried, repeating to myself: "She was inside me... She was inside me."

I repeated it as if to summon that moment over and over again, but each attempt grew more and more ineffectual. It was like a spark, a glint fainting with its own anticipation. I could not summon her presence no matter how much I tried. I cherished that moment...

Yes, she had loved me, and to someone who has never been loved, it was overwhelming, not only to be loved but to know that this love is of equal preponderance in either soul... We had loved each other, if only for one precious moment, but nothing had ever happened between us, because we had to run away from each other out of fear.

The poignancy of that moment would be forever deluded with my own affliction. After an hour of weeping and tearing out my hair, I beheld the ominous book: "1984."

I flicked the pages randomly and fell on the following passage, a passage I hadn't yet read, but that taunted me in a way that only destiny could achieve:

"For a moment he had an overwhelming hallucination of her presence. She had seemed not merely to be with him, but inside him. It was as though she had got into the texture of his skin. In that moment he had loved her far more than he had ever done when they were together and free."

The crazy thing is… it happened to me before I read it. Yes, it happened *before* I read it.

How was that possible…?

It was after this moment that I knew I was going to commit suicide. For the first time I thought I was actually going to do it, and the "moment" was only moments away. No one can possibly know what it feels like to reach that point. Simultaneously one feels an enormous sense of horror but somehow, you look forward to putting an end to your suffering. For a moment, I thought, this is how it must end. It can't possibly end any other way.

I had to kill myself…

CHAPTER NINE

Most people live their lives in reality, or what they perceive to be real… and not imagined by their sconces.

I've lived my life almost entirely in my own mind, and it has tasselled dreams and nightmares that I should only dare to tell you anonymously, for fear that I am mad. I am convinced that I have been implanted with a microchip for several years now, but it's only during the past eight months or so that it has caused me irreparable damage.

Was I crazy or were these things really happening to me…? There was no way to tell, no reference point whatsoever. It was like an invisible testimonial against my own dharma, and the heavy traffic in my mind was always in reverse… an abyss into the satoris of hell: the path to illumination.

It's quite intrepid to meet yourself in the future without knowing how to control the present without sheer volition, but some things are not so penchant to retort and parry forth with truth and experience… the present moment is eternal within each of us, even though it seems to fail us every moment of the day.

You should know by now that I am an absolute failure. I've failed at everything that I've ever endeavoured to accomplish. And so I've always worked measly, low wage jobs that would leave me starving. So I would always fall back on my ambitions, trying to graze by as a nomad. Could an individual like myself obvert the Government, and the Illuminati… solely by exposing it?

***

I was a bit of a radical, but mostly in my youth… I was a Socialist because I had a bad attitude, and I had a bad attitude because I was a Socialist. But the older I got, the more I became conservative—out of vogue with the rest of society… I call it the

"Atlas Shrugged" factor. I finally understood Conservatism, and even more so Libertarianism. The more you accomplish, the more money you make. It makes perfect sense: it's all about the individual. It's all about freedom: the more freedom you have, the more you can pursue your own happiness, whatever it may be...

It's all about free will...

"Individual ambition serves the common good."

I was a Libertarian because I wanted to be successful yet open-minded at the same time. You see Socialists think that society should adapt to them as a group, but the reverse is true for those who truly understand Capitalism. You have to adapt to society... in order to become successful. Some say that Socialism is neighbourly, but I would rebuke you to say so, because your neighbour can take care of himself, can he not? Is he ineffectual and recumbent? Do you think your neighbour to be inept and bungling as an individual? Do you find this to be neighbourly?

Yes, I long wanted to live in a nice middle-class neighbour-hood with a nice car, and a beautiful wife---maybe a couple of kids. That's how you acclimatize your ego to your personal circumstances, like an intellectual peonage. You see, ambition nourishes the spirit... If you have intelligence and ambition in a society like this, you can accomplish just about anything---it's called "Capitalism: the Un-known Ideal." If we were to establish Socialism tomorrow, all the successful people would disappear: all the artists, the athletes, the CEOs, the innovators, the restaurant owners, the entrepreneurs. They would go live somewhere else where they can be free to prosper as much as they like...

The economy would collapse as it always does...

You see, people are at different levels, we are not equal. If we were equal, we could revert to Socialism without fanning its rep-roach against the spirit of man. But Socialism takes away your ambition to better yourself as a human being—both financially and spiritually. It destroys your aspirations, whether you're an artist or a business man.

But if there's one thing I love more than material things, it's knowledge: the more you learn, the more you earn. It takes intelligence to succeed in a country like America, that's why people risk their lives to come here…

There's a reason why all the poorest countries in the world are Socialist, while all the richest countries are Capitalist… really think about this: poverty is an attitude, a state of mind, not just a circumstance imposed by the Government…

Here is a simple anecdote for your reproof:

"There was a professor at a major University who decided to treat his class like a Socialist society. He decided to give all of his students the same grade no matter how much they studied, no matter how much they fared individually. The average grade was a C. And so he gave everybody a C after each exam. The A students were really disappointed, while the F students were really happy with their grade. After a while the A students stopped studying altogether, simply because they would get a C no matter what they did. What was the point of studying? That's what Socialism does to your spirit. It takes away your ambition… It deprives your impetus of its stakes, which can be as high as you want them to be as an individual. You become a lazy ne'er-do-well…"

Yes, Socialism makes everyone equally poor due to hyper-inflation. That's why I consider myself to be a Libertarian… I'm fiscally conservative and socially liberal. Are we not all individuals? Are we not all harbingers of liberty…?

Indeed, you cannot force people to be equal.

Heil anarcho-Capitalism!!!

***

The real reason I would work these menial and outright droning jobs as a labourer, like the annals of a library as a clerk, and the archives of a pharmacy as a stocker and a cashier, wasn't so much that I was languid and somnolent in my wake, or that I didn't want to make something of myself, but out of wanting to make *too much* of myself. I was a starving artist… the kind of artist who truly believes in his own aberration, no matter how much they reproached me with their consequence---the penury of ignominy.

The problem is that I'm never satisfied with anything I create, because once I get into a project---it develops so fast that it ends up overlapping itself over and over again, like the broken wheels of a jalopy on a thruway.

I start to learn so much about what I'm doing that, by the time I've done it, it's no longer germane to me, nor effectual to the errands of my soul. I work and toil to the point of perfection… and it's a tough grind to subside into the ego like an Orwellian bootjack. But, in reality, it's just a relapse into a deeper snare of consciousness, by which I morph my own identity into a Cyprian aerie, to take the flight of fancy one last time---the idealistic notion of an indiscernible aftermath in the mind of Satan: the Apocalypse.

It's like raiding an empty house for ingots of the spirit, the proverbs of aberration… the unknown ideal of Capitalism, and thus Libertarianism…

As an artist, I've done it all only to wind up with nothing, like Ginsberg's "America." I've been a painter, a poet, a writer, a singer-songwriter, and yet I've been none of the above simply because of my overambitious, encyclopedic mind.

For a while, I was even a physicist, trying to uproot the sum of all equations to explain the Universe, which I will show you later…

I've always believed that when a man comes to know himself completely, he will have known every other man in history by default. It was like a perestroika for the soul---a crown of thorns for expediencies of all sorts, which corresponds to its own Martello in the twilight of the gods.

I always dreamed that somewhere out there, there was a secret society that was filled with people just like me---madmen, artists, philosophers, poets, revolutionaries, bohemians. I don't know why, but I've always felt this sharp pain in my heart… like a thorn in my indolence, which then welters its own torpor.

This just added to my problems and to the burden of my mission… but what God was asking me to do was insurmountable, it was monstrous, unfathomably evil, like carcinogen in the spirits of my endorphin's stockpiles, which I cannot refute on the offset. We are against evil in others… save ourselves.

CHAPTER TEN

While I sat there, contemplating suicide again... I remembered something that would completely derail my plans like an invisible train...

I remember when I was twenty-one years old, the first of these unfathomable events presented itself before me. I was briefly living with my sister, Angie, her fiancé, and my beautiful niece, Desiré. We lived together in an apartment next to a graveyard with the scene of the crucifixion in the middle. At the time I was working on my poetry book and had just finished writing a poem about John Milton's faith in God in spite of his blindness. The poem itself had gotten too convoluted to even mean anything but I finished it nonetheless and decided to look out my bedroom window... what I saw would change my life forever.

I saw a dozen little black birds looking for worms in our back-yard next to the fence... And I would have moved on with my life without thinking twice about it, if it wasn't for the fact that one of these birds was perfectly white. It was of the same proportion and species as the other birds, but it was white. I was so astonished by what I saw, that I actually asked myself out loud: "Why is that bird white?"

I couldn't believe my eyes. I went to the bathroom to have a closer look to make sure I wasn't just seeing things. The white bird remained among the black ones. I stood there for a few moments, getting chills up and down my spine all the while. Then I heard my sister walking toward me from behind and I looked at her with what must have been the most perplexed face she'd ever seen.

"What's the matter?" she asked as she held Desiré in her arms.

"Did you see the birds?" I asked.

"Yeah, I was showing them to Desiré a minute ago... Why?"

I found it impossible that she didn't mention the white one.

"Did you see the white one?"

"The white one? No..." She looked out the window and reacted as anyone else would, with utter perplexity and awe. She even went downstairs with her digital camera and tried to film what was happening but the paranormal activity froze her camera—a brand new camera. And as she took the footage, I remained upstairs with John... I explained to him that in virtually every country in the world would consider this as a sign from God. And as I explained this to him, my sister overheard me coming back up the stairs and said: "That's crazy... I prayed for a sign from God last night."

"What kind of sign...?" I asked.

"Just that He exists..."

"Well... there's your sign," I said, almost delirious with every possible emotion that you could imagine. I went back into my room and looked out my window, and the white bird was gone, even as the black birds remained. It had appeared sometime after my sister had shown the flock of black birds to my niece, and it left as soon as we discerned it as a sign from God... having inculcated my mind with God's grace for the remainder of my life. I immediately got down on my knees, and repented for my sins. I made a promise to God: that my Art, in whatever form, would always be a testimony to the truth.

At that moment, I had become a sort of invisible priest, serving god amongst the gentiles. Everything I did from that moment on would be for God. If it hadn't been for that day, I'd be an atheist... or at the very least an agnostic.

CHAPTER ELEVEN

It took me the better part of several years to write, record, and produce my album on my own---I recorded the second half in two weeks in my room at Hotel Chelsea. !OKARMA! was finally finished. And the theme was perfect---the death of Postmodernism! I hated Postmodernism, and I was glad it was being morphed into something else altogether: Metamodernism.

I released !OKARMA! on an extremely small scale, but it would still have an immeasurable effect on my life, and the events that it would clinch would completely deteriorate my sanity. I had had an interview with a local magazine that had gone well, but never got published, for reasons that I can only speculate.

My coworkers, however, had reacted to it in an extremely positive way. I thought that its release would be fairly uneventful, and in a way, it was. But in another, it was eventful to the extent that I was not able to handle the amount of attention that it was getting me. People were acting very strangely around me… and I couldn't understand why. I decided to ignore it, but it would eventually get to the point that I could no longer flout nor contravene against it.

Something big was happening all around me, and I couldn't tell what it was. It almost seemed that everyone around me knew exactly what was going on except for me!

***

About a week after that I went to visit my father in downtown Greenwich Village. On the drive over my sister, Angie, was talking to my father's wife, Mary, about how the governments were planning to put microchips in people for the New World Order, the world Government. I couldn't hear most of what she was saying because of the ringing in my ears, so I mostly focused on entertaining my four-year-old niece, Desiré.

When we got to my father's house, my sister made me watch "Zeitgeist" on her laptop to show me what she was talking about in the car. I watched it and found some of it was truthful while some of it was spurious. Just another person trying to take control of what I think and feel. I pointed out that the narrator was discrediting the Bible, and yet fulfilling most of its prophecies, like the mark of the beast: RFID---a sku on the forehead or the right hand: 666.

The Image of the Beast---Baphomet as a societal pariah on a giant telescreen, demanding worship or death...

My family and I had a brief conversation about what was happening in the world at the time, and how 9/11 may have been a plot by the United States Government to instil laws on people by tugging on their fears---Socialism was thereby the endgame.

At one point my father said he was appalled, and I implied that perhaps the Government wasn't just planning on putting chips in people but were perhaps secretly doing so already, which made him jump out of his seat: "Whoa... Paranoid!" I found his reaction truly disconcerting: he almost jumped out of his chair, as if the Government were listening to our conversation at that very moment.

That's what the ringing was for... they could eavesdrop on all my conversations with their supercomputer, their CPU.

"I don't know... I feel like there's something in my wrist... and the ringing in my ears sort of sounds like a computer going through my brain in a straight line."

"Maybe they're trying to shut you off..." he said jokingly.

I said: "Maybe they're trying to turn me on..."

What if that lump in my wrist really was a microchip and it had recently been activated... Was I asking too many questions...? Was this a new way to punish and castigate subversives?

That night I smoked a joint with Jason and we sat down to watch a movie, but the ringing in my ears was so bad that I decided to go to bed early. I thought smoking pot would alleviate my suffering, but it only enhanced the frequencies to an intolerable extent. As I lay in bed that night, the ringing in my ears started to fluctuate in all sorts of different directions. It was so painful that a few times I thought that maybe I was dying. It was like a flagrant Isthmian fixture in my soul that I could not confute…

I truly felt as if my brain was shutting down, and that they were sending signals into my abdomen and into my heart with their super-computer. It got so bad that I began to squirm and fidget in my cot. The pain was surreal, and it didn't help that I was high, because now my paranoia was really getting the best of me, like a bestial shunt, a jolt into my personal shunpikes in the eventide. It was like a super-natural force in a parabolic concerto come to life in my own mind… decubitus.

The next morning I took some Aspirin, but they did nothing to mitigate the ringing in my ears---nothing ever would. It was here to stay… But I thought if somehow I could get rid of my "cyst", it would stop: if it really was the source of the computer sounds in my brain. The problem was that the doctors were Government workers, for social health care, and they were taught to declare people like me insane if they even hinted at the possibility of having been micro-chipped by the Government. But this was only the beginning of my descent into madness, like melting clocks: the Persistence of Memory.

***

When I got home and went back to work, people were still acting very strangely around me, but this time it wasn't just my co-workers, but also the customers. And some of these customers had special rings, rings that bore the compass and the square, to be specific. This was especially strange, because as soon as the ringing in my ears had started, my first thought was that it was a signal, and I had an unusually strong urge to join the Freemasons.

Once I even had two Freemasons standing at my cash. I greeted them like normal customers, but these two men, for some reason, started whistling the same song in perfect synchronicity without even saying hello. I thought that maybe it was a Masonic hymn… a mantra for the initiates:

The world is in pain,

Our secret to gain…

I tried to go on with my day, but these Freemasons just kept on coming, one after the other into the store, showing me their rings in subtle yet obvious ways, like asking me to help them find a product, and then scratching their faces to let me see the rings from my own coign of vantage, which was apparent to them as well. They knew who I was… and why I was here.

"The awaited one comes late…"

Was this Nostradamus' allusion to the Freemasons? Had I been invited to become 'one of them,' to become immortal with the rites of their resurrection?

Or was it just my ego again…?

At home, I almost always had my face in a book, and I had hundreds of them on my book shelves. I had consciously decided to figure out what was going on in society… I was determined to figure out what was going on once and for all. I noticed something that I hadn't noticed before about my books. Some of them had a symbol on the back, which consisted of a triangle, and three letters: ΔEAN.

I decided to separate my books into categories to see if they had something in common, but I couldn't make a connection. For a moment I thought: I'm over-thinking things again. What I didn't know was that I had stumbled on something big…

It was something that could potentially get me killed…

At the time, I had made a friend at work, who would always talk to me about what was going on in society every time I went to his apartment to smoke pot with him. He talked to me about the Freemasons and how they had signs and symbols, and how American money had subliminal Masonic messages printed as an outlier. He also talked about how human beings used to be thirty feet tall, and that the real reason the U.S. Government had gone to Afghanistan was to cover-up this fact, so as not to confirm the stories in the "Old Testament." Our conversations just added to my paranoia. Something was going on. I needed to know the truth… because I thought the truth would set me free.

I was dead wrong… the truth would ruin my mind.

CHAPTER THIRTEEN

The more I looked into the truth, the more it destroyed me… and yet the more it destroyed me, the more I needed to know: believing in my heart that eventually the truth would lead me to my digs and billets---my ego's reprise.

I wasn't interested in money, sex, and power… I wanted to know the TRUTH!

"The truth will set you free…" I said to myself.

It would eventually alienate me from everything I had ever known to be real. The ringing in my ears was driving me insane. Sometimes I would sit alone in my room and beat my head with my fists, but it did nothing to joust against it. I had felt this way ever since I had moved to Greenwich Village, because when you're a single mother on welfare with a child, and a low wage job, the idea that life ever gets better is a fleeting one.

My demons were asquint to my own ration, and yet they were so much stronger than me at the time, that it wearied me to think that my life would never get any better. In my mind, I was poor, ugly, and stupid, and no matter how many times people told me the opposite, I never believed it. I had a distorted view of myself, like an anorexic in front of the mirror… and nothing would ever pull me out of my depression, not even Abilify, the strongest drug on the market.

I got on my bed, like a foetus, and cried to myself: "I can't tell which thoughts are mine…"

***

As a student of Humanities at New York University, I was so poor that most of the time my fridge was empty… I spent all of my money on books and CDs, like some kind of peripatetic---a nomadic bohemian on a quest for truth in the arts. But it was all for naught… I grew so desperate for money that I took my friend's offer to hide his gun under the planks of my sink for a thousand dollars. He was my drug dealer, and, even though it felt wrong, my excuse was that I didn't have a choice. I could've used to money to pay off my debts, because I had many debts, but I just needed to get away to recoup my sanity…

Not once in my life had I done something out of the mere volition to do it. When you're poor, your life is: wake up, work, sleep, wake up, work, sleep… So I decided to take the thousand dollars, plus my vacation money from work and go to Old Montreal for a week to go to the galleries and museums in the metropolis by myself. A friend of mine had gone to Los Angeles, and he had rented a hostel bed for a month and a half just to get away from it all.

I remember, when he was my friend and neighbour in Campbellton, we were playing Legos in his basement…

Suddenly, his sixteen-year-old brother came down the stairs and said: "Stop what you're doing and listen to this…" He put in a cassette in the stereo called "Nirvana: Nevermind."

I remember listening to the whole thing from beginning to end without saying a word, or even thinking a thought. Something in me changed that night. It was that moment that I decided I wanted to be a professional musician: like Kurt Cobain, my first idol. I was only eight years old at the time… even then, I felt like it was my destiny.

Later on, when I was ten years old, I bought a cassette with my own money. It was "Nirvana: Unplugged in New York." I listened to it every night before I went to sleep. And it made me fall in love with the acoustic sound, which is why I wrote !OKARMA! as an acoustic album…

CHAPTER THIRTEEN

Meanwhile, things at work just kept getting stranger still, more Freemasons roaming and roving like itinerants, and more customers pointing me out and saying: "That's Him... that's Jesus!"

An old lady even came to my cash, without buying anything, and said: "Thank you for taking our 'calling.'" But the adulation wouldn't last very long, because I had no idea what I had gotten myself into, or how I had done it... but I knew it was big.

An FBI agent had even come in to see me, and asked me stupid questions with a fake Mexican accent. He had an FBI hat and shirt, and he made damn sure that I saw it. There were even two government vehicles in front of the store, surrounded by several other FBI agents.

I wasn't entirely sure what was happening, but I knew *something* was happening...

I thought: 'Oh fuck... There really is a revolution going on... and they know it!'

There were even two black government vehicles parked in front of the pharmacy... possibly waiting to take me away at a single sign of deferment---simply to abjure me as a dissident: insubstantial as it seemed to me at the time.

Were they controlling my thoughts with HAARP...? Could they control my mind in the same manner that they were controlling the weather? Were they trying to scare me, or were they trying to push me forward?

And so I decided to go pay my friend, Calvin, a visit after work, and talk to him about what was going on: how Freemasons and the FBI were visiting me. I knew that he knew something more about it than I did. He started talking to me about these shape-shifters... and I said: "Yeah, but that's just people talking about things that they don't really understand." But he was talking about it as if he knew it were true... which was really disconcerting. I thought: 'Is this guy being serious? That's the scariest thing anyone's ever said to me…'

Then, his step-father came upstairs to have a toke with us. He then joined the conversation and said: "Well, it's the shape-shifters who control society…" And he went on talking about these shape-shifters in a harangue for about fifteen minutes, but I couldn't focus on what he was saying, because I kept seeing myself in my own mind giving Sieg Heils from the top of the Vatican's loggia to hundreds of thousands of people.

Now I was really getting paranoid…

Did this have something to do with the ringing in my ears? Had I been micro-chipped by neo-Nazis? Whose 'calling' had I taken? Why me…? Why was I so special…?

Questions were swirling around my mind, like diabetic vortices, but none of the answers betided me as I obliged them to my most infernal doubts about society. Shape-shifters, neo-Nazis… whatever was happening, it was starting to scare me.

I remember when I had first told Calvin about the ringing in my ears, he gave me a look that seemed to say: "You're under the radar, man." Later in the night, we were talking about the revolution, and he said: "We have to shut them down, Solomon…"

He was obviously talking about the Government---it was a putsch against Capitalism, a Socialist take-over! A foray of ethics and principalities unlike anything I'd ever seen…

These shape-shifters were behind the "Synagogue of Satan."

"I will make those who are of the Synagogue of Satan, who claim to be Jews though they are not, but are liars---I will make them come and fall down at your feet and acknowledge that I loved you…"

It was on my walk home that things started to spiral out of control. I was thinking about all the things that had been happening to me, trying to make some sort of connection. It was during this moment that I could no longer tell the difference between what was real and what was not.

What was happening to me!!! I needed answers… even if it

killed me.

"1984"

Was this book a factual account of how society really worked? Was Big Brother a real personage, the CEO of America behind the scenes…? Were we living in a dictatorship, an autocracy without even knowing it? Was Freemasonry the escape? To become 'Free and Accepted'? Was any of this real… or was it all in my mind?

I was breathing heavily, as if I had just run a long-drawn-out marathon…

Yes, I was insane, it was official, and it was the ringing in my ears that was causing it. I fiddled around with the "cyst" in my left wrist. It felt like a computer chip and the ringing in my ears truly sounded like computer frequencies. Do I know too much? Are they going to kill me if I divulge their secrets?

I decided to read further into the book, desperate for answers, and I read yet another passage:

"And all the while he must keep his hatred locked up like a ball of matter, which was part of himself yet unconnected with the rest of him, a sort of cyst. One day they would decide to shoot him…"

Now my paranoia had instilled itself into my mind, like a sickening perigee around my conscience. They knew everything about me… all of my secrets would be divulged. Sleeping had now become a perilous undertaking, not just because of the ringing in my ears, but also because they likely had the ability to induce me with specific dreams. I was an android for the Government… and they were trying to brainwash me into becoming an ultramodern Hitler. Were they going to shoot me if I did not comply, nor obverse their behest? Was I predestined to die as a martyr to my own cause… to forfeit my destiny to the stars of Aquarius for nothing but tinsels and sequins in the eye of Horus?

The microchip… Can they see through my eyes…? Hear through my ears…? Were they already chipping people to monitor their thoughts with HAARP and MK-Ultra…?

I went to the mirror and looked at my features… 'No… it can't be…' I took off my shirt and looked at my right rib… It looked like it had gotten pierced a long time ago---indented by some kind of lance. Then I looked at my back: scourge marks! Where had these scourge marks come from? How had they gotten there? Perhaps they had been computerized into my mind, and they were not there at all in reality. How could I tell…?

What kind of mission was this? Had they chipped me knowing who I was, or was I being brainwashed into thinking that I was Jesus of Nazareth, to establish the New World Order? The world Government…?

"To us a child is born, and the Government will be on his shoulders."

Was I really working for INGSOC in the Ministry of Truth by writing this book…? Was it the Freemasons who had 'called' me…? Was I an unwitting, modern-day Ayn Rand for the Illuminati…?

"Should you really be working at a pharmacy when you're on a mission? He knows I'm saying it nicely…" a woman had said to me from the other cash to my left. Later on, a man came to my cash with a hat that said JESUS on it. He made sure that I saw it… tilting his head toward me without saying a word, as if he were bowing in his obeisance to me.

When I got home, I quickly grabbed my Bible and started to browse through the "Book of Revelation," desperately seeking answers:

> "'He also forced everyone, small and great, rich and poor, free and slave, to receive a mark on his right hand or on his forehead, so that no one could buy or sell unless he had the mark, which is the name of the beast or the number of his name. This calls for wisdom. If anyone has insight, let him calculate the number of the beast. His number is 666.'"

My mother had been right all along…! She wasn't crazy after all…!

I went to the mirror in the bathroom and looked at my face. I pulled my hair back. I even looked like Jesus… there was no doubt about it… but how could I tell what I really looked like…? Perhaps they had altered my features with the computer chip…

How much control did they have over me?

I had taken their 'calling' after all. Was this what they were trying to get me to do? Put microchips in every human being so that they could be controlled in the same manner that I was being controlled?

This is what it feels like to be microchipped by the Government. You can't tell the difference between what's real and what's not… it's like being in the "matrix" by yourself.

I got down on my knees, weeping, and tearing out my hair in a fit of madness, a pique of soulful displeasure, trembling and shirtless in my room… begging God to have mercy on me. "No!!! This is wrong thinking!!! This is wrong thinking!!! Stop these thoughts… now!!!" I took a deep breath and got down on my knees. "O God, don't make me do this… please, don't make me do this."

Suddenly I remembered the scene from the "Passion of the Christ" where Jesus had done the same thing… begging God to take the chalice from His lips.

I sat down on my couch, contemplating what to do…

I looked at the planks beneath the sink… For the first time, I was not merely thinking of committing suicide, but I knew that I was actually going to do it. For a brief moment, I felt an instance of exhilaration, as if I had found the answer. I thought that perhaps if I committed suicide I could be free from my pain: nirvana.

I got down on my knees and said: "Please God… please don't make me do this…"

Desperately I crawled on the floor and pulled the plank beneath the sink...

"Dissemble no more!"

The gun was in a black zip-up bag. I pulled it out and unzipped it... But then I thought better of it and decided to go to the hospital.

I had to get away from the Government… I thought that maybe I could get my "cyst" removed. Even if they shot me… it was worth the risk. So I went to the hospital and waited in the waiting room. But the doctors look at me adversely and refused to take it out on account that it was in the hands of my family doctor. Could they not tell that I was suicidal? Did they not see how distraught I was? Then, I recalled… they worked for the Government. They know who I am, like that woman and the cashier.

No matter how I looked at it, I was entrenched in madness and despair. The revolution was happening in my head... Whatever it was, I didn't trust it. What kind of revolution requires you to have an electric current going through your brain 24/7?

Either way there was no way to prove to anyone that any of this was actually happening to me, no matter how consistent it was in my mind. It was the kind of revolution that was impossible to prove... Because all the evidence was in your head, and you could easily be dismissed as insane by other members of the Government.

CHAPTER FOURTEEN

The next day, my coworkers at the pharmacy were still bombarding me with my own stages of hypomania. They could even transmit their thoughts to me and had done so the previous night, telling me that "this is our Zeitgeist!"

One of them, as if he had witnessed my debacle the previous night, said: "Don't commit suicide, Solomon... the world's a better place now that you're here."

It was coincidence after coincidence, a barrage of hopeless correlations: synchronicity. I was like an ecumenical apostle to my own ideals, simply to ideate this kind of reprimand against myself.

Later in the day I went to the cash office, and one of my female coworkers yelled: "This is our 'Zeitgeist,' Solomon, we've been over this!!!"

They knew about the shape-shifters!

'You're crazy...' I thought. 'No, I'm not...'

Later, I was standing by the receiving desk and the woman standing next to me said: "I have to go see Dr. Hussein to get a cyst removed." Were they talking to me in codes? I thought that maybe this doctor could remove my "cyst," maybe he's aware of what's happening, and he could help me. I could finally get rid of the micro-chip! Are they talking about my "cyst"?

The delivery man for Old Dutch passed by me and said: "Shouldn't you be doing something...?"

Another young girl came to my cash during her break and said: "Aren't you supposed to know everything?"

I replied: "I used to... a long time ago."

And then another co-worker said: "Hey, traitor..."

To which I replied: "I don't control these things..."

I left work early that day to go to my guitar lessons, and I told my guitar teacher about how I felt like I was remembering all sorts of knowledge about the pyramids, and the way the Universe works.

And he suggested that I read a book called "Initiation," by Elisabeth Haich.

I then told him that I thought I had figured out the Universe. And he said: "Well... I hope that for your own sake and for the sake of the rest of the world that you do have it figured out..."

'What does that mean...?' I asked myself.

He knew something that I didn't. It was almost as if everyone around me knew what was going on except me. I thought for sure he was a Freemason, and he had been given the task to recommend this book to me by the hierarchy---the templates of society. But I was not going to take their blood oaths before I found out the truth about this so-called "secret society." I had gone to the Masonic Temple a few times to talk to someone, but I kept getting a sinister feeling in the depths of my stomach when I entered the Gothic-like edifice, with an owl above the entrance, along with the compass and the square in plain sight...

I'd read a few books on the subject and it seemed just fine to me, at least on the surface. They were a rather chivalrous fraternity of Shriners, but then again I'd also read a book titled: "The Deadly Deception," by Tom McKenney. It explained unequivocally that the higher degrees of Freemasonry are Luciferian—that Lucifer is God. They even had the symbol of Baphomet, proudly worn on their hats for the higher degrees...

Here's what Manly P. Hall said about the Craft: "When the Mason learns that the key to the warrior on the block is the proper application of the dynamo of living power, he has learned the mystery of his Craft. The seething energies of Lucifer are in his hands and before he may step onward and upward, he must prove his ability to properly apply this energy."

I'd also read "The Protocols of the Elders of Zion," which is about a plot to enslave the world through the New World Order... and I thought it the be true. The goal was global Socialism under the reign of the Antichrist. That's why we need to be wary and recognize the Antichrist as soon as he comes on the scene. He is currently waiting in the wings. But the people with their names written in the "Book of Life" will recognize this dignitary as soon as he hails the

New World Order, from his gubernatorial place of duty… with signs and lying wonders to deceive even the elect.

I also read "Morals and Dogma," by Albert Pike, in which he envisioned three World Wars, the last of which would lead to the demise of one-third of the world's population and the rise of the Antichrist. It would be a war between the West and Islam, which are both controlled by the Freemasons on either side. It's money laundering at its worst, and all started with 9/11… which was also orchestrated by the Government for a strict and diabolical purpose.

He also stated the following: "To you, Sovereign Grand Inspector General, we say this, that you may repeat it to the Brethren of the 32nd, 31st and 30th degrees:

"The Masonic religion should be, by all of us initiates of the high degrees, maintained in the purity of the Luciferian Doctrine… Yes, Lucifer is God, and unfortunately Ado-nay is also god. For the eternal law is there is no light without shade… for the absolute can only exist as two gods: darkness being necessary for light to serve as its foil as the pedestal is necessary to the statue, and the brake to the locomotive. Thus, the doctrine of Satanism is heresy; the true and pure philosophical religion is the belief in Lucifer, the equal of Adonay; but Lucifer, God of light and God of Good, is struggling for humanity against Adonay, the God of Darkness and Evil…"

They even shake hands with dictators and popes, because they all share the same agenda, the same schema of arithmetic: the New World Order, which is also purposely Christless… and there's only one way out, if you should so recognize:

"Two women will be grinding with a hand mill;
One will be taken and the other left…"

***

Later that night, I suddenly got the urge to explain the Universe, and I started working on it immediately. Stranger still… I felt as if I actually understood it thoroughly. I suddenly knew all the equations and all the formulas, like the Koide formula, the Larmor formula---as well as the theoretic foundations of General Relativity and Quantum Field Theory. I was remembering my knowledge. And so I started writing it down as fast as I could. Yes, I felt like I was remembering my knowledge from all my previous lives, in the same way that the scarecrow in "The Wizard of Oz" remembers his knowledge when he touches his ear and says: "Oh boy, the Rapture! I've got a brain!"

I can't help but remember the end of the movie, where Dorothy gets into the air balloon. On the balloon are the words 'State Fair,' but if you reverse it, it says 'Fair State'...

I thought for sure that it was a reference to the New World Order...

***

Meanwhile, it was as if my physics book had been downloaded into my brain by the computer chip in a split second, like lightning in a bottle.

The ringing in my ears!!!

And so I wrote it down as fast as I could on my laptop...

As soon as I asked my first question as to how the Universe worked and sat down to write what I remembered from my past life in Atlantis... my lights began to flicker. At first, I thought nothing of it, and I went on with my hypothesis.

I thought that there was something more to this flicking of the lights. It seemed as if the lights were only being flicked when I asked specific questions... and at times, I felt as if there was a presence in the same room as me. I put my hand out and asked the spirit to touch my hand, and it felt like static on my skin. There was definitely something in my room that wasn't human.

I stood up and said: "Wait a minute..." Just as suddenly the radio stopped... The woman speaking on my radio was silenced, as I stood there debating my mission.

I then spoke aloud to the spirit and said: "Wait... Am I crazy? Or am I doing God a favour?"

As soon as these last words escaped my mouth, the radio

started just as suddenly as it had stopped. The spirit had somehow stoppered its electrical flow while I debated the inherence of what I was meant to do, as a favour to God, to promote his insights to modern man, like some kind of Cyprian prophet...

The revelation poured out of me like ticker tape... a helix for which I had to hunker down at my escritoire, like a discomfit for my cognition.

CHAPTER FIFTEEN

By the time I finished writing my physics book "The Principle of Equilibrium," I'd had several nervous breakdowns, and I had to live with my father for several months to get a grip on myself. I had also gotten my hands on a copy of the book that my guitar teacher had recommended me. It was about a girl who went back to her past life in Egypt to learn about the secrets of the ancients. And somehow... I already knew what the book was about before I read it. At one point it even said that I had been 'accepted' into the Order.

This is the paragraph that I read earlier that day:

'And today, this curious coincidence with the book. Coincidence? No... it was a message... a message! Even the most skeptical intellect would be silenced in the face of so many coincidences! No, I could not doubt it: I had been accepted!'

She also talked about the powers of initiates, from Moses to Noah to Abraham to King Solomon, from who I begot my name.

Apparently the human body has seven levels of consciousness, which are also called chakras, and only initiates have access to these dimensions of self-parlance. I understood that during initiation, they conduct an energy into the spinal column, to illuminate the seven chakras one at a time.

The reason they keep their secrets so secret is because they are so powerful and dangerous that, were it given to people who are unworthy of it to begin with, they would use their power for evil in the name of God, causing cataclysms, earthquakes and epidemics all over the world.

She even talked about the buzzing in the ears for the chosen ones, as some kind of global awakening... as a symptom of ascension, which I refused to acknowledge, simply because it terrified me to think about it.

Was this an invitation or even a 'calling' from the Freemasons to establish the New World Order as some kind of Masonic

Christ…?

Up to that point, I had read three books about the freemasons, and in one of them it said that, though they do not recruit, if it is indeed a special circumstance, they do sometimes 'call' to a person…

Was it at all possible that my 'calling' had come from the Freemasons…?

"The Moon in the middle of the night…
The young sage alone with his mind has seen it.
His disciples invite him to become immortal…
His body in the fire."

I wanted nothing more than to alleviate and assuage the suffering of the world, but they were preventing me… It was against the law and I understood the reasons why. It was against the law, because if I could teach others how to do these things---the Governments would be losing too much money for their gross domestic product. The pharmaceutical industry would collapse. There would no longer be any need for their pills, and people would lose interest in their propaganda, and thus become enlightened by the truth. The Governments did not want people to realize their own spiritual potential here on Earth.

We were slaves, after all.

They wanted to efface God once and for all with their secular "Zeitgeist," so that people would never be able to learn the truth about themselves, to make them forget Atlantis forever, where God once lived in accordance with man---the concords of an eternal symposium. The objective was to put microchips with a sku in every human being on Earth, simply to keep them on a low frequency, so that they would never learn that they have a spirit to awaken in themselves like a chi. That was the true objective of the New World Order. The microchip is not just to control your bank account, it's to control your mind, as I have experienced for myself. I walk this path so you don't have to. I am here to prevent them from accomplishing that goal, for fear that God would pour out His wrath on these ignorant and rather loutish people.

When they finally establish the New World Order, the leader, the despot of the world Government, will be the Antichrist. And the lost and the pitiful will follow him all the way to the gates of hell like unabashed sheep---the abomination that leads to desolation.

When someone conceals the truth---especially the Government ---it's because they're seeking to have power over you, which is why Jesus said that all manner of sin will be forgiven men, but "those who speak against the Holy Spirit will not be forgiven."

It's a direct offence against God to conceal the truth, because God gains His power by revealing it, while the Devil gains his power by concealing it.

The economy was completely reliant on the sickness of the people... They wanted to make you dependent on their solutions, on their pills, on their ideologies, on their mortgages, on their very way of life, because as long as you were dependent on their way of life, their way of life would persist for the ultra-rich, and the Illuminati.

Had the Government written the Bible? Had it been written by these shape-shifters? By the Freemasons...? Were they brainwashing us with religion and politics... movies, sex, and pharmaceuticals like Zyprexa, and Clozapine...?

***

The next thing that happened to me was even more frightening than everything else combined. But I still couldn't tell whether or not it was real, or if it was the Government trying to get me to do their bidding... or if I was experiencing the longest psychotic episode of my life. I had gone to visit Calvin because he was the only person I knew who actually understood what I was talking about. But he talked to me in codes and ciphers, so it was hard to tell what he meant. When I left, I got perhaps a few hundred meters from his house, and it was then that the Government sent me another message.

But this one was completely different from IAM=AMI, this one was truly horrifying.

Somehow, they had managed to completely reverse my own

mind on me… and made me see a brief vision of fire falling from the sky. The implication was that God was going to destroy the world with an all-consuming fire.

As I walked across the street, I thought that it was them. They were trying to get me to do their behest, to enjoin their bidding, and I had to resist.

How can one trust a revolution that requires you to have an electromagnetic shockwave going through your brain? After all, I knew their philosophies well, having read their dictums in Orwell's reverse "manifesto." They believe that to get someone to do their will they have to make them suffer. I just hoped to God that the ending would be different…

Did they not understand that I was trying to spare them from living in an Orwellian dystopia under the reign of the Antichrist?

***

Later, I took the bus the rest of the way home, and I sat at the back next to a girl I had once encountered at the New York library. I was so preoccupied with what had just happened to me that I didn't notice her at first. When I finally looked over at her, I noticed that she had a swastika drawn unto the cuff of her pants with a permanent marker… as if she had known that I was going to take the bus with her that night. I had to look at her pant leg several times to reassure myself that I wasn't just imagining it.

I thought: 'Do you seriously have a swastika on the cuff of your pants…?' She immediately looked at me with a stern face, as if to say: 'Do it! Do it now!'

I immediately looked away…

I knew she was listening to my thoughts, and so I sullied her with my temperament, like a post hoc eleventh hour…

***

When I got the mall, I sat down to wait for my next transfer. And while I waited and pondered what was happening to me, I happened to sit next to an old man. I briefly thought to myself that he was a shape-shifter, and as soon as the thought entered my brain, he stood up and started to whistle. And I swiftly looked at him and thought: "You're a shape-shifter?"

He casually nodded and continued to whistle as he walked toward the entrance. Then I looked at the old lady who was sitting behind him and thought the same thing toward her: "You're a shape-shifter!" She slowly turned her head and looked in the other direction.

These reptilians don't like to be seen for what they are. I looked at the old man again, and he briefly shifted into a reptilian in a most menacing and portentous manner. Somehow the letters on his hat shifted into greenish letters that spelled out: "Obey SS." Then he shifted right in front of me. It was as though he had changed dimensions.

Suddenly his teeth were sharp as ancient conodonts...

I was terrified---scared out of my mind. These creatures were really here, and they controlled our society from top to bottom, like a pyramid.

In fact, they had made the pyramids...

CHAPTER SIXTEEN

I was becoming more and more reclusive, because of all the things that kept happening to me whenever I went out in public, but I still needed to find out the truth about my situation. I decided to go to the Barnes and Noble to investigate a few things further, and what I was about to find out would only further confirm what I already knew.

They were here… and they controlled everything from the economy to the Government to the media. We've been enslaved since the beginning of time by the thirteen bloodlines of the Illuminati, like a systematic monarch: since Genesis.

While I walked around the bookstore I grew curious about the symbol that I had seen on the back of certain books: ΔEAN. I looked behind every book I picked up, and there was no longer any doubt that this symbol was only on the back of books that were either written or translated by members of the Illuminati---INGSOC. It wasn't a triangle, it was a pyramid.

And each degree was 60 degrees, which summons the notion of the 666 once again.

But there was one book in particular that bore the symbol ΔEAN that made me feel sick to my stomach: "The Satanic Bible." The Synagogue of Satan. These shape-shifters were in charge, and they were here, hiding in plain sight---like a Postmodern exhibit: derring-dos of spiritual omniscience!

Was this yet another delusion? How could I tell…?

***

Then one day, me, my brother, and my father went to the shopping mall downtown. We began to walk around the food court. After a while, my father said: "Let's let Solomon lead the way." And so I took the lead… then I thought to myself: "You're following Hitler…"

My father and my brother both coughed at the same time. They had heard my thought loud and clear.

We soon entered HMV, and while I browsed I saw a DVD called "V." It was about reptilian humanoids trying to enslave humanity as a lesser race.

My father said: "How else are you going to know what they're planning?"

And so he bought me the DVD and we left HMV. After we did this, I saw an old woman that looked like a reptilian shape-shifter. I leaned forward and said: "Leave the fucking planet!!!"

In my periphery, I saw my father and my brother jump into each other's arms, as if to celebrate the revolution. My dad then drove me and my brother home. He then got out of his truck and grabbed me by the head.

"Don't get rid of the buzzing in your ears…" he said.

Later, on Facebook, he sent me a message that read: "What's that buzz, tell me what's a-happening…? What's that buzz, tell me what's a-happening…?" This was from the movie titled "Jesus Christ Superstar." The message was simple and clear… and my burden was overwhelming by now.

Another time, he said to me: "The world is waiting for you, Solomon…"

Is this what schizophrenia feels like…?

Is it simply a misinterpretation of reality…?

There was no way to tell.

And so I isolated myself…

***

I remember sitting in my room, watching one of the Government's Hollywood propaganda films… It was then that the revelation came to me: "The Nazis won the war?" I immediately covered my mouth. I thought that maybe they could hear me. That was the purpose of the ringing in my ears, after all… to remind me that they were omnipresent, and that they had complete control over me. I was the perfect candidate for their Manchurian objectives. I had always been a solitary young man, a loner.

The Government knew a lot more about the Universe than they were divulging. They were working with aliens at Area-51.

But there was no way to prove it. It was impossible to prove that I had been wronged, because the doctors were in on it, the entire town was in on it. It was as if Greenwich Village had been modeled specifically to fulfill the task of establishing the "Image of the Beast." Hitler's face on a giant screen in the middle of Time Square, reading his speeches over and over again. "The Triumph of the Will."

Their one-eyed symbols were everywhere: 666.

I thought I was in a modern-day concentration camp, wherein you could not tell what it was unless you had the intellect to do so. We were slaves…

The problem was that I could no longer tell what was real, and what I had intended into the world by my own delusions. Was it all in my mind? Was it kind of like being colorblind…?

I had even written the book about the Universe that they had intended me to write: "The Principle of Equilibrium."

'Thank you for taking our 'calling.''

I had seen various people around me looking at me as if I was the grim reaper in the guise of a cosmic Christ, and confirming that I had received the message by evaluating my reaction. The revolution was in my head… but it was real. The people around me were lying to me! The liars! My own family! They were all in on it!

It was like the Truman Show… wherein I was the narrator. And I could do nothing to obtrude it.

In fact, one of my mother's friends, after running across her in Greenwich Village, spoke to me for a few minutes and then said:

"You've suffered enough… it's like the Truman Show."

It was like Big Bother in reserve… it was as though everyone could see me instead of me seeing them…

It was eventually revealed to me that it was not ear damage… Hitler himself had had the same thing happen to him. He had a ringing in his ears… And now it was all happening to me. I could see myself giving the speeches in his place. I could see myself becoming him. 666. Hitler: "The Image of the Beast."

But there was a possible escape… to escape the system, you could join the Freemasons. You could become 'one of them,' a secret society of artists, athletes, actors, politicians, and they controlled the world from behind the arras, like Polonius in a labyrinth of knowledge, where only the knowledgeable can find themselves interned in the pediments of Hessians, like the resurrection of Christ, where wisdom is buried by the acquittal of God.

The Great Architect of the Universe.

There was a subtle recruiting system in place that most of the population was too obtuse to perceive. You could be free… but in order to be free, you had to indulge in their system, which requires most of the population to be slaves, to be ignorant of the truth.

You could join them and all your dreams would come true. If you wanted to become a famous artist, they would make you famous. They were the puppeteers, they could pull all the strings. I knew that I had been accepted, because a friend of mine had given me the book. It described what it meant to become a Freemason. But there were rumours that the Freemasons worshipped Lucifer, that they sacrificed children to Moloch, that they were the evil of all evils, controlling the world from behind the scenes---some people even thought that they were working with an advanced civilization of reptilian humanoids from another constellation: Draco.

I had uncovered something about society that I wasn't meant to uncover. The Freemasons had even visited me at work, divulging their rings and threatening me in subtle yet obvious ways.

Yes, I had been invited, but as long as I was not one of them, I was a threat…

***

Later that month, I happened to have a very interesting conversation with a 32 degree Freemason at my father's house, an old friend named Allen… and we talked for almost an hour about the New World Order and the Illuminati among other things.

Apparently, Freemasonry and the Illuminati were two

completely different things…

At one point, he told me that the Freemasons had the Ark of the Covenant hiding somewhere other than in the Holy of Holies…

He then explained to me that, though I had read many books on the subject, I would never be able to crack the code…

"You'll never figure it out if you don't join…" he said.

I asked him if there was any monkey business going in on… or if it was true that they worshipped the devil, or even Baphomet on a floating pedestal made of sackcloth.

He denied it rather passionately and fervently at the same time, thus stymieing my presumptions…

He assured me that was no dubious activity going on in Order whatsoever… and that it was all based on the Bible, which caused me to take a respite in my conscience…

The conversation led me to believe that joining the Freemasons was the only logical explanation for all the coincidences happening in my life… though I still had a few reservations about the whole thing.

Furthermore, at one point, I showed him the story about the white bird, and as he was reading it, he called me Hitler three times…

"Hitler, Hitler, Hitler…"

It was all very disconcerting and confusing at the same time, but I was also very curious about becoming an initiate.

I thought for sure that it was the Freemasons who had called me on that fateful day… and that I was nothing more than a Masonic Christ in disguise.

In fact, in one of the books that had I read, it stated plainly that, though they do not recruit, they do sometimes 'call' to a person if it's a special circumstance… as crazy as that all sounds, even to my own presentiment.

Up until this point, I had read four books about the Freemasons, and in a few of them the author in question specified that every character in the Bible, from Moses to Jesus Christ, were all initiates… because they were called initiates as early as the pyramids of Giza, with a history of more than 3,000 years…

Apparently, the initiates would have visions of the future, which is why the pyramids have hieroglyphics of helicopters and airplanes engraved into the walls.

They only began to call themselves Freemasons when they established the first lodge in America…

I think it was in 1717…

Whatever the end to the means result would be or rather *should* be, I felt as if I had no choice but to join the Freemasons and take over the government… to thus establish the government of God on planet Earth forever and ever… as the Bible specified.

'To us a child is born, to us a Son is given, and the government will be on his shoulders… and he will be called Prince of Peace… of increase of his government and peace there shall be no end…'

'He will rule them with an iron scepter… He treads the winepress of the fury of the wrath of God Almighty… and he will dash them to pieces like pottery…'

Whatever happened, all I wanted to do was the will of God!

And if joining the Freemasons was part of my journey, I was more than willing to follow through and discover the truth for myself…

'The truth will set you free!'

***

It all begins with a dream within a dream. In this dream I was in my room at Hotel Chelsea, and I went to touch the television screen… my hand went through it like an ecliptic lochan.

And so I reached in further… and further…

Suddenly, I went through the television screen altogether and found myself in Amlethus, a town where everything was in black and white, like a fascist cartoon. There I met an ominous character: Lucifer. We were sitting inside a lighthouse… it was obvious that he was the head of the Illuminati's monarch: festooned in gems and charms.

And so he began to speak, as if he were trying to enlighten me. And so I sat there and listened to what he had to say to me as intently as I could…

LUCIFER

A subconscious hell awakens in me every
night, where sardonic trees speak of yester
night's dreams, and a maiden's ruche is on
the biblical whore of Zion: it's like a hillock
made of auras in the Oregon countryside;
and yet I cannot reckon my own nonsense
without it! It totes me up like a poetaster in a
paddock for equestrian metaphors that
traipse across the Universe like an unknown
zodiac. And so death strolls on every
sidewalk like a spectre with a scythe, and
life is a movie in which no one knows the
plot. Meanwhile, vanity sits on Goliath's
throne and condemns its own naivety to the
floor… yet hatred is an old witch in a castle
made of jasper---hell is just a place where
curiosity denounces its own asperity…
You're a blank page in the book of
knowledge; and oscillation is the opposite of
artlessness; wherein memories are just
moments that keep trying to get back at you
like Hamlet's effrontery against time…
wares of omniscience for falderals at ease
within themselves and each other. It's like a
shoal of dreamless medusas, which
acquiesces its own yoni in the deep love of a
sumac… Wisdom is a possibility made
declivitous by one's own shovel in the

heath. Fear's a tyrant; and no tyrant wilfully surrenders his post; the post must be overthrown, not the tyrant. It deceives you with the dukedom of its Orphism; like a cataleptic animal in a Cathari full of bees; wherein love is like a hypocrite's bougie---in the skies of Atlantis, whose subconscious wilco inhibits its will to power like a sloven. It's a ghetto whose politics is one-sided and impartial; it evolves from an eft to a newt, like an ego's ideal, whose eyre seeks Ezekiel's wisdom in the grave. It's like a Trismegistus matrix for masons in America; a Hesperus twilight of the gods; a Mesopotamian panorama for the sane…O false electricity in the rains of Sudan exploits a Machiavellian intelligence on its own turf… by dint of its own past-iche, its own resolve… like an insincere mystery foregone in "Paradise Lost"… wherein I was the villain. I told you the truth, Solomon; you wanted to know everything, and so here it is… Let your mind do whatever it wants, and live out your id like a Nietzschein god--- a pre-exilian man with his destiny written in the stars! Literature is just an old disease with new symptoms in each passing century, like a Modernist gauge for the ignorant, whose metaxy is stubborn as modern maths to Plato. The Book of book's jargon has no device of ascertainment to befuddle the institutions of knowledge; no reign over my senses to overhear themselves like peek-a-boo soliloquies; no traffic in the intellect, nor on the smooth notion of poetics; no sapience of enigma, nor intrigue of spirit to

ratify my own destitution---these
vulnerabilities are not extant without me in
the Vulgate. These are the absolute denials
that leave me obdurate in my stool. Am I
wanton to reject nobilities that do me no
overhauls, nor calm my dejections, nor
muddle my ideas about time and the span of
a pretender's Achilles' heel---which is to
pretend…? To me life was a dreamless
spool, approaching nothing truthful, nothing
to realize or venture toward; only an
undeterred sense of hyper-theology and
desuetude awaited me at every turn---a reel
in the conscience of God. But who, honestly,
can understand the intimations of logic in
the "Western Canon," the distress of skies
unrelated to the happenings of the human
quo?---in a world wherein the little black
orphan blinks but doesn't see; where the
Dark Lady smells the brood of providence in
the foo; where unprincipled animals prey on
something that makes them prey to
something else; where a maharishi is at once
happy and indolent in his berth; where idiot
sinners keep striking the temple wall that
will crush them; where well-tricked
assumption stumbles into the room where it
will disappear and return mysteriously as
knowledge; where women despise the
objectivism of their mirror; where one man
dies and walks into another man, and
another man dies and disappears, and
another man dies and ascends to heaven, and
another man dies and falls into perdition.
Don't doubt the life of a man in a grot, if the
darkness provokes him to the light. But it

won't cloak your madness with so ghostly a charge, unless you've given your fears to the past, and made the future suffer to speak the rite. Your dwaal, forming an escarp in your mind, has taken the shape of your memory, to think itself a more powerful presence, like an incubus on a dais… And now your errantry's been drawn into the diligence of man, to make him admire his own mind by exploring yours, like Shakespearean espionage. Who's aged along with his wisdom like Dante's "Inferno," which proves as halcyon as a cataract, whose irony cannot touch its own meaning. You are in a lighthouse in search of God… The fortuneteller's tarots were not within the breach of her chaps when they eye it not in single spies. The broch secludes the Holy Ghost to its own interim; like the eulogies of literature, whose quantum summation needs an Apollo-like acumen to resolve the pice to nil, which espouses the prescience of its own metaphysics like a grave. Literature is dying like a black-and- white flick about dystopia, wherein truth assures its insight like a prisoner in a Postmodern gulag. Are you too impassioned to be rational or too rational to eat the entremets that await you at the tables of hell? My insistence is the bigotry of your storm lantern… Art thou not a gorb of illusions? How conclusively the outlook of your insight, with a scornful firth as the mind's egress, seeds the schema in the huddle of concurrence… Is it not like the rose's theocracy, which sustains the salt of the earth, as though they were not buried by

the mystery they intended to hide within the
grave? It advocates the burial of God, who is
dead within me; O it obverses no beauty in
the shucks of incidence, but would rather
scorn love's most fecund embryos, whose
emotions shall not grow when circumstance
enfeebles the elixirs of its passion. O it's
what elides my heart, Solomon; and it seems
feasible to the capricious bogglers of the
One-eyed Merchant, who utters his bloody
riposte to stymie their oblivion with war and
famine. Though he understands what flags
sweetness in wine, he is still misted by
forsaken virtues, which never again shall
bestow the grapes of wrath; and thus, it's in
such a heart that I find my patronage, for
though conscience does not feather our
resolution like a crow in heaven---our
regrets might endure what must be
understood as a misunderstanding. Thus, to
achieve the gofer's pride and the goodwill of
his ordinary insights, sagacity weathers what
cannot be known by the molt, and dawdles
no more the hilt of Lo's subconscious prose,
that the egger thereof might verify her
orations as the luxuries of truth in the palace
of wisdom... O love is but a common
rhapsody exchanging knowledge for
something less obvious than the obvious.
Life is a metaphor: a gambol against nature;
one must not be distracted by the event, but
find the revelation that hides within the deep
like a sunken flotilla---an armada's coulee in
the desert. And yet you, with your purpose
integral to its life, must redact whatever
makes you revise yourself anew. What is it

that beckons dementia to its post but to yarn the very effect of cognizance? Man is in defiance of himself, suffering like a nutshell with a labyrinth inside it, as though its travels wrote themselves on his trimmings, not the stables of his memory. Promise me the stars, and I'll stall the constellations with a glance; give me a tributary for my psalms, and I'll catch an eel with my bare hands… It's like a novelese held together by dooks and branches... an Abbasid monastery; a Paleozoic orchestra that never ceases to abjure its own Poles'ye; a polemic against Obadiah… Self-love, of the ego, is like an obituary for dead intentions. At times it abhors its own existence, like a pageant for our monstrosities; an Abu Simbel whose will abstains its own acanthus on your ego's tomb… Poetry is like a subconscious Aceldama against its own beliefs; a meridian opera for Hottentots, which houses its own stupidity like a prodigal roommate; a manga about a Manichaean hypomania. O it caters to its own presumptions like a cither full of uncertainty. It launches its metaphors into your mind like an onager; a hellbroth for its own grief; a griot whose grasp on reality is as far-fetched as a merlot full of inklings. And so I grok my own Draize test with Shakes- pearean irony---like an exordium about the end of time. It hearkens to the voice of God, like a Jacobean interstate to nowhere. It's a Luchullan feast for Crowley's ghost; a subwoofer for the outlaws of a Piltdown man---Aesop's crow reveals the truth! It's a Pindaric ode to its own repute; a seltzer full of unknowable paradigms; a bishop whose diesis is estranged by its own sui generis. It's a Sukkoth for pro tem gravediggers, under the aegis of take-no-prisoners politics. It's like a tithe for the mascot of timeworn duplicities; a tug-of-war quodlibet that tunes out its own aria; a Bullamakanka for poets of that ilk. Schizophrenia is like a whirlwind of hasty metaphors… and irrational cosines in the mist… And so I'll scamper love's lessee, when destiny's elderly stars master my expeditions to Atlantis, though it'll be as vexing as Sisyphus to the castles of Corinth. I'll have a chinwag at this averment, to scythe the gumption that adjudicates my literature's prettiest chasms in Xanadu---like the modern bookworm's inferno to unleash the dogs of war. It's like hamming the meal before revenge is ever served, coldly or not---that the prodrome of our soulful illusions might not rig with the intellectual prods of our nature in the pokey. I was not trained in the academes, and so it became my gambit by force of indulgence; not for beauty, no, never for beauty. And so you scrimp my poetical ordnance by skiting about your magnum opus; yet, like a fearful sprig, you deny that Lolita sleeps in your neighbor's house on Derby, plucking your super-normal predilection of its silver-tongue, as though sense could no longer teach itself so common. It's not my cause to discourage your ambitions---whether they be a poet's vanilla-like discourse, or a lover's ligature in a hearse. Pleonastic fluxions flow more clearly with the rainmaker's prayers, when he sprinkles powerful irony upon the ocean, to make effluent its satirical streamlets back into the mind of God… It's like a chook that understands the cine films of a madman--- Dali's Avalon; a jalopy's fixer-upper in the reins of a fool; the Paraclete's despair; a midnight hotel. The truth is simple, Solomon, like a sea nettle in a cottage, which captures its own abeyance through its fascist windows; a Frau, indeed a Fraulein, whose power subsumes its own Manasseh. It's like Odin's pragmatism against his own Oedipus complex; an off- Broadway synthetic; a post hoc, ad hoc fantasy; a perique in a flue that transcends its own permutations. It's like a psy-ops against the future of corporate America; wherein a marsupial Socialism awaits the upheaval of the plebs; a novena for the oscillations of Meta-Amlethus---the death of Postmodernism… It's like Oswego tea for the vain; a politburo for Pollyannas haunted by the poltergeists of Scrooge; a Pyrrhic assumption that love is nothing but a dead man's dream, whose vendetta is all but subsumed by its own lien… Shall you jalouse my gentle doom, if I skive my complacency and persuade my tenure like an infinite jest on a bookshelf? It's love's lethargy; and yet our dreams cannot be disclaimed by loveless exhortations, like the acropolis of God, which shines upon the truth like a messianic proverb about Hell… When heaven sleeps it dreams of this---our self-made macrocosm is, like an over-

weening doocot, as civil as self-pureed
blood of a dead bird---whose exothermic
oblivion is coldly preserved by the sculleries
of its provincial dust. Beguiled by truth's
agnostic sleep, they pine for clever
neologisms---which, like the Neanderthal's
Modernism, became discovery's highest
precedence against poets, whose worthy
escapade puts a hoop on the means of its
own vigor to slow the pith. My mind pules
like a sook in Amsterdam when I think
about it. Proud men may pray beneath their
helixes of defeat, though their dogma
advocates didactic self-sympathy, like a
Sufistic soogan in the rain… I always
thought that the kingdoms of my splendor
and the eventides of my dull assumptions
met at the bight like a binary. Yet you
cannot say this quean's a concubine, whose
gudgeon is so well kept within the secrets of
my book, that no wisdom knows her for her
premise, her patine---she's the empress of
my Elizabethan, cyberpunk dreams, as
though her potency could rival a fear, even
when the danger's as unexpected as death to
immortal storytellers. Their words would die
if only they knew my stories were exacting
the deceptions of my ion; ay, they'll never
forget my inklings, not by trades of
ascension, but since he suffers all by
thinking nothing. If pain endows its own
circumstance, is not its circumstance made
helpless by its own cause?---while it pulleys
the tongue at the carnival, as though profane
ears could prize the glops of our most
abysmal diktats, like a goblet full of dead

worms. What do the dead dream about, Solomon? Dreams are sleep's honesty; the dead man's sleep is celestial, eternal. You must meditate as one no longer in discussion with Chaplin's shoons. Let truth author your thoughts, like a rose that grows backward into the ground. All truth perishes in its assumption that man can understand that its provenience is forsworn to each cue, like Santeria about the Yobura's proverbs. It may last a season; but for a book to be a marvel down the ages, it must show mankind the troubles that even a spiritual age cannot disarm, nor dream away the providence of self-love. These memories do me dungeons, they beautify the crypt I've sworn myself to in these frills of conscience; for time often hastens me to my clock and cockcrow--- since it's they who suffer it as cunningly as a helot musters the Sun on rainy nights, in the electric forests of Amazon, which kindles its own archetype like Dylan's guitar… And so I would simply ward it off like everything else… by ignoring it as fair dinkum. Do not believe in your own diocese without a discothèque's omniscience over the prowess of your wonder. For fevers would neglect their own dotage if it brought them to their poetics without pause to consider the day--- to succor a life wherever it may borrow the usage of the All-Seeing Eye, not to make men ill but to use their blood as carriage to their purpose. Ambivert be my business in another's mind if the heave-hoe tops the mindless pursuits of relativity---like gravity's rainbow. Is this the ration you

speak of, even as the fishbowl cannot
legislate a fish, or the fen an alligator, or the
tree a jackanape? For truly what defends us
keeps our fears as near to our ration as a
galanty show, a bayou in the subconscious,
though our minds predict it by its poverty.
Tell me God makes my ration keel, and I'll
dance to my own conceit, like a do for
gentiles. It was like an invidious poet, whose
faith is miserly to the Knox---a neo-
Malthusian's precept. It's like an olio's
prolix; a reiki, whose datum is make-believe
and nothing more; a Scaramouch, who
forgets his wisdom like a Zoroastrian priest,
an invisible sequitur; a flux capacitor, which
mechanizes the human mind. It's an
irrational constant; an Isolde that morphes
itself into a nimbus full of atomic raindrops,
wherein Nirvana excels its own laureate to
the life of a literary oarsman. It's like
Oberon's obiter dictum---it preens my
psychosis, like a pitiful genus that forefends
its own hylozoism; a hypergolic flame that
dares itself against the Sun. It's like a
Hyperion's dissolution, which glozes the
temperament of gneiss; whose gnomic
passado hoicks its own holocaust on the path
to Hell. It's like a poet's lotus of identity; a
lovelorn matinee; a matzo's preterit against
time; a mazurka that internodes its own
botany like a hinter. It's a Flemish feast for
poets; yes, it cogs my logic, like a logo's
oath to Communism in a free country, which
emotes its own ambit like an empyrean
rezone. It's an excursion against an idler in a
cheap motel, whose infernal destiny is like

an infinite pool, whose influx is like a fiery
phaeton; Satan's venire---Poisson's ratio,
which nodes its own efficiency like a no-
good nik; an Abyssinian academe for the
wicked… And so winter drubs my hope; and
with such a glum hanging on my sapience
like "Portrait of a Lady," and a hush on my
offences---how may I obverse the duple
cries of my guitar, when it's the song that
has made it such a skit on my sadness? O
God! My mind is split into halves... And so I
cavil the sage who argues with my ration,
that I'm nothing more than a cockatoo on
the asymptote of the Universe; that I was
nothing more than a comfit full of enzyme, a
dossier full of sarcastic pressures. And so I
fibrose my most flammable interjection and
set fire to the terms. My love's enteric, like
the butterfly effect on wisdom; a word
struggling to become its own meaning to the
invisible. Does that make me a bigot or a
saint? O does a sine compute our stubb-
ornness when we give banquets to our ears
where wisdom has no seat? Does a cloud
make our throes of conscience heap their
own thunder on the hosts of Sodom? To
fight the pavilion of post-mortem
inquisitions, as though the Sun could set its
rays on whimsies, and spurn reality to its
pain, is indeed the satire of eloquence. Thus,
unkempt belief, down-at-heel, in self-
thwarted thralldom, trudges among sunlight
yet un-filial to its font, since such a society
would idealize its slavery---but none shall
know what drills the conscience of a rose,
like an awl; until it cowers against what

denatures its growth. Uncertified through the
sufferance of change, naivety still could
confine the scent of heraldry by ignoring the
stint. But it's a regret to none who know that
antonyms seek opposition to strengthen
themselves, like the gross indignation of
winter's tales in the summer time lilac. O
how nature presumes its own presumptions
to be true in the quirks. Such a man would
only denote his mind like a zephyr instead of
cajolery at a steeplechase—he would not
barter with a demon to jape himself like a
fallen angel---a jaunt for the disciples of
Christ. It's like a birdless cage for entropies.
Were I to convey to you all the perjuries of
my love, maelstroms would bethink I am
become Jupiter's elixir, a utopian sycophant,
whose dialect is flung unto others as God's
catharsis. There's no strath from here to
death---from death to here; so don't abscond
from your grave to a life of worthless riches;
the earth judges no man according to his
estate, it can only take what is flesh. Now,
come, Solomon... so far your mind's been on
the puddle, but within one mere dimension
of knowledge; why leave them flat as a
plain, plain as a square, square as a swing to
a jazzman? You'd drag me through the
depths of hell and gently sing the lauds of
angels like a thief in heaven, with nothing
but sacrilege in your testimony... If you're to
gentrify the kismet you disperse on the
gambler's table, shouldn't you bridge these
chances with your knowledge of the
diversion? It's to climb to the unknown by
what we know, and await your death to

know what life keeps hidden in its casket
like Apollo's elegy... Let me number the
roots: you have eyes to covet with, hands to
kill with, to steal with; you have a tongue to
lie with, to take God's name in vain with; a
brain to scold God with or worship another,
you have the means to dishonor your parents
with; you have tasks to disrepute the
Sabbath's day with. Tell me, what God
would scold our sins, though he provides us
with the faculties that make our trans-
gressions attainable? Indeed, regret is an
infection that serves its own discretion.
Corruption bows down to the crude
conscience of honesty, and its end rises to
replace what it once worshipped. Thus by
your indecent accord, I'll suffer the abscess
of fortune; the false fulfillment of gluttony;
the slavery of lust; the foolishness of envy;
the asinine self-importance of pride; and the
counterproductive troubles of sloth? Such
happiness is as false as Apollo's Wake
among the Danes. A fool's happiness also
demurs his stratus like a fear-gripped
plenum... The alpenglow is keen, like a
synagogue for the nabobs of your wisdom...
Drugs allowed you to become baneful with
no questions asked, like a Druid in his own
nol-pros; the Tree of Knowledge in the
pampas of Nok. But the spirit cannot
possibly sin against itself... because nothing
outpaces its own velocity, and no one
outthinks the truth. The mind is just what
confirms reality as a predestined gridiron of
possibilities, to be discovered gradually and
confirmed as forever plausible to our senses.

The ringing in your ears, Solomon---it's a global awakening, and you must lead the way! It's a state of fugue for the easily forgotten; which compiles its own destitution like an alley cat's dissertation about Freud; a firkin for the lost, whose logic is like a steenbok's Logos; an ohm's respite against electricity. It's a Meistersinger's melancholia; a pauper's reproach against the parables of Christ---a Rhaeto-Romance for the politically incorrect; a dirge against fat cats and skinny puppies. It's a mirage for a dark horse---fathomless, like a fatwa on the head of a publican; it's a Faustian reciprocity against Fauvism. It's a lichen from off the tree of knowledge; folk art for the digeratis, and the future of futurism. O it's a hoopoe's Alger, which leaves its legacy in the asylum, like a fascist apropos. It's an apsara's bipolar lullaby, which dreams of its own Masonic initiate; like a pro bono work of literature against the sane. It's a Samsonian magnum opus about a mezzanine's Apocalypse of inner-thought; a mercurial toper's silent suicide---a Rabelaisian streak of luck. It's like Shakespeare's posthumous intaglio, whose intelligentsia is a thruway into the past, which peeks into the epigone's mind like a cassava. O it helms the incurrence of hell; a bell jar's omniscience into the Plath effect; I am fully indemnified. Mankind is damned, unloved by the politics of estragon, and here I was like a prideful recreant, expecting everything to come my way with nothing in return, and so I professed a certain indictment of the spirit. My life had been nothing more than a brooding of unlikely parallels of pain; we're all ghosts just waiting to disappear, intelligible to the eye yet ever stricken by a certain blindness when pain appears to disappear. It's like a yakuza for the illiterate… Think you this is but a doggerel's prose or something more akin to our mortal verdict? And so I, a reeler of past proclivity, must redact my tears as though they reefed my riddles, which acclaims my faults like an ancient sorrow, an alcove for the ghosts of Byzantine; O it welts its justice in what forsakes us to clamber to our graves, and yet Sisyphus vies to attend our conclave. You are too fateful, auspicious, Solomon; fate is never kind to its own realm, like the Egyptian Oz… It carps our ophidians and patronizes our comprehensions---for hypocrisy draws subsistence from its own integral passions. So shameful to the prophet's timeworn skews are the spectrums of his conscience, that his doubt broadens his epiphany like a grave. Is there no deferral in a madman's philosophies that shall dissuade his gibbet and sweeten his exuvial rose? It's an Orwellian escapade against the plebs, who jaunt their destiny like a frozen fire. O it taints my uxorious dreams with utopian tropics, slinging my blood on whatever the truth abjures against its own affidavit, as though slaughter were the response to calumny. Its dowdy élan is weary with fate's gawking sunsets, wherein false equanimity transmits its own knowledge into the mind

of Apollo… Words can amble in their own
precinct and be criticized by the rains; so let
unworthiness decree my pavilions like the
rains of Sodom. Would you gruff against a
matador; challenge a monkey to a chess
match? O pride slakes the zodiac serenity of
God to a deeper poultice than a stream of
blood; it bridges the lacuna's pause, to see
your senses where gravity bends the light. A
lighthouse, burning by the fiction of its own
light, cadges for censor in the ashes of a
holocaust. Who then will fictions maze,
when brainstorms crow you brighter than
any light, more hot than fire's oath…?
Indeed, odds and inklings cannot translate
occurrences; what shelters his reform
worsens his scotophil, whose pain polishes
the scripture of his decadence, and covers
the trials of his comprehension with the
dove's petticoat---the analysis is dead,
though it could never overthrow a star's
cavalry with a snowflake seeking eulogies in
the astronomy of atoms… No flame is
submersible in the ides of winter; a
snowflake cannot threaten a star… and so I
coop the corollary, wherein truth is a cupel
for the blind. Vanities as angelic as eves of
conscience thwart my distractions like the
One-eyed Merchant, whose deception edicts
my ignorance, like a child who does
discourse with a dead-fallen butterfly---
whose words, unruffled by their claims, pass
their poetical pause within love's most
shameless drawls. And so I preen the
polemical angst of all who bear the truth in
their wits and wiles; it's intelligible not to

strive against it, yet decadence makes meets
at events unwonted by their holy share.
Fiction slithers into the interstice of love and
makes us hew the pursuit from the follower
---anxieties speak like wontons in my
whims; they make mealy literacy engross
interpretations, more apt to disavow their
traducement than question their gauge? It
breeds the hegemony of Elysium. I
remember the hue of disaster and the blush
of annihilation that fawned my fathom,
colder than Pluto's dish, to become no more
a virgin to soulful ragouts, when fiction
slaughters nightmares to the Frisch, like
Isaiah's nutshell, wherein subtlety elucidates
complexity, and simplicity digests the
monocle's temporal multi-cultures of
insight… Indeed, no larrikin should caper
the road to wisdom with his monistic
eloquence, beautified by truths that defy
their own conveyance, whose assessment
argues no abasement into an angel's ecstasy,
like a fearless sot, whose pastoral patience
pilms his intellect. O it mafficks his travesty
like a meaningless sermon about Metamodernism, which feagues my foehn like a
bogey in the dead of night. If I sleep within
the meaning, wake me when the words are
dead… yes, it's what teethes your volition,
whose ambrosial sport is as theosophical
squibs chatter in the ears of Postmodern
tribes, who have never seen those noble
earthworms in Hamlet's grave. It's who you
were meant to be, Solomon. The recourse of
hyacinths bears its burdens like a priestess in
the moonlight, by which no coaxial notion

grows… though the serfdom of my intransigence bellies no disaster. They dare away serenity and then call it devilry to snook at a nova! Let it do what undoing does! Angels and ministers of grace offend us! O crude inspection of the well that beckons no echo; what kind of science usurps liberal wonder to squander the intelligence of a snail darter? Vile be our rotes, shame be our inference; the wriest slander sports no season to dock a substance when the throe of time sends futurity aback, like a thyme honed to pull the roots from the toiler's heart, to spur the growth life rues in such a mead to his imagination? O levy the matter like a bore, like a choof, a poetaster, misplaced like a garden on a baleen's back---the drachm, the burden of the voodoo chufa, is to sadden what cannot cheer his good spirits, like a quay that bears no ship to the wheezes of the sea---but a wise ship avoids the rugged waters. Words, though precisely crippled, will see how a poem's meant to walk, for in their shame, what they labor for will worsen their augury, the past, now in the flesh, will seem more considerate of the future's boons---does the auger bore your mind like a bilge on the Acheron? I am a master of deceit, a rigger of truths and fantasy; and yet I'm adumbrate with anxiety. It's as predictable as a psychic's life…but don't gamble on a crag, you'll follow your dice to the sea to know whether the wager was worth while, even as the wager itself fritters your life. It's a falderal of conscience! It's like the yard goods of your epiphany. Is he

so bold as to formalize a fork and tell me
what he eats is the plate's vengeance against
his stomach's cotillion? My God, rose, thou
art sick! Thou art falser than a dead gobble
whose gook is now the pedigree of your
confusion. Is this another one of those
rabble-rousers who soaks my dithyrambs
with a necessary mesa of incidence? A
lascar would sink his boat to define it with
his lies, even as his lies cause him tot sink;
but mine… mine is at such a level as divinity
upholds in the purposes of guilt. Is it larceny
to feed an oversized leviathan when it could
be served to such a god? The salesman
cannot see the altar of God as a chamber of
secrets, until it convokes in his vanity, since
to worship such a vanity is to make it holy
by the recognition of your own passion. God
took me to the edge of ecstasy and closed
the gate, as though my fevers convened in
the brothel beyond it. Are you a ghost in a
husk of life, pretending the hangman favors
you by the origin of his compassion? Do you
think life favors its recreants? I'll assure you
no refrain of this; sith this diatribe's a fable
to you, and sith you refused to believe its
provenance was love. You've strained the
diapason of a seraph and held choirs to her
ears to make her weep at the prejudice of her
insight. If my love could sing, cognoscentes
would garrote themselves like angels in a
dead end. This gambado of lust and love,
passion and confusion, error and ecstasy,
would lure me to a madness I could've never
expected for myself; it was as pronounced as
a ghost to an ill-fallen house without

windows to let in the light… It's like a pia mater for soulless durbars; a scuffle hoe that denies the steed; a dynatron's fantasy; a garda's daydream, wherein Durham rules on its own constituents, which Platonizes its Puseyism… like the rite of an Aquinas; Durga's targe against its own Ivy League impressionism. It's a Jack-a-Lent with no knowledge to aestivate. O Apollo, whose Wake is double-Dutch, sustains its own two-faced gadroon, like a molecular sieve for criminals, whose mote abstains its own menagerie. It's a palatine for obtuse maxims that surround our mind like runaway palfreys; a philippic against the parliaments of Rajya Sabha, whose secrets are betrayed by its own deceit; a Falstaffian guilt trip, a Shakespearean loggia full of Gullivers ad nostrum. You're out of your mind if you think the truth is like a Laputan dream; a skeleton key that opens the doors of your subconscious. It's like a Parnassian's snafu, which condemns the sanctums of your innocence, which forgives what you haven't done yet… My soul's tropology, like an invisible troubadour, was the focus of my failures, since my tropic tears would putrefy my desert's ode to the emptiness inside me. But Pavlov would not say so. Would he shrivel his oath to time like a dying rose in an aster's ford? Don't let the tears evolve without the froth---the scullion trusses you like Minos on a settee… a Reuben's hypothesis about his own reveille from unsettling dreams about a cockroach's bureaucracy… I'll drop the eaves even on he who beguiles me to my infinite jest! A poet! Than to you, I am no more invisible than a sad man to his mirror. Does it spill the feelings into the proper cup; or does the cup spill its troubles to the floor. But you have missed the illusion. Double the pun; double the meaning. Don't be a prem to the pedantry, if the birth is your Confucian ego; for then the mechanism perishes in your Pooterish disclaim like an iodide… And so I archaize the saunter of every truth, like a tale too policed by structure to seek authority in a theme, or liberty in an idea; it's like a puna for the meek. It's the death of Post-modernism! Apollo's Wake… Have we not booked our figurations with enough lore to accouter a mermaid with the scriptures of the deep? O we parasitize the pratfalls we owe ourselves, when they seem the prankster's eulogy, which would prawn us toward the schism of our conscience when the ocean performs our wails like palestras made of indium—it misunderstands us all sometimes, or is it we who heard it wrong? What think you of this society? Do you detest it, abhor it? Have you witnessed its pogroms and gainsays in your soul, so that now your soul, through art, dares to leap upon the age and tell it how what is mortal within us is the disease to all that is eternal in our spirits? Would a ferret 'scape its hole to know the darkness wasn't real? I'll baptize you a pretender for now, and your twinges will despond their recreation in the epic of a Metamodern siesta. I'll squire you to a rood, and wassail at your tomb like a hypocrite. Do we quarry the twinkle of a snapdragon, when the dew deplores the very ascension of its cloud when it reclaims it? Shall we become the desert to understand the Sea never was so deep as to discourage the rumors of a prophecy? Shall we relate every tear of a tragedy to he who is more remorseless than a pirate at a play, who eyes the templates of a gush with dumber scold than a feather's hitch to scaffold the nightingale it once adored? Life is the idea of death enamored with the mirror of time; do not seek an echo in a clock that spurns the moments it also stifles… Love is like a Japanese quince; a trogon of resolution; which I cannot reclaim without some form of secrecy… It's a Hadean inquest into the soul; an Obie for your offstage pretensions; an homage for your delusions of grandeur; a Frise aileron into nothingness, even as the fainéant involutes into thin air, like an Orphic warbler; which occludes your paranoia from ever becoming real. It's an adhocracy for Adi Granth---whose palsy haggles its own encomium, like a Buddha's Panglossian that prevents knowledge. It's a prima donna's abstraction against graffito; a Egyptian tomb's pre-Socratic sense of humor; an insulin shock into the anthers of my subconscious; an Eleusinian mystery that peers into its own naivety; it's a Dispersion that sanctifies its own enigma, like a deathless Butskellism that never ceases to forgo its own epithet; a matrix for Markov's chain of events; the poetry of a Neanderthal, whose sapience is Napoleonic to the nth; a spiritual bouquet; a Wheatstone bridge that wheeches its own velocity against the passage of time. Indeed, it was like an eon that enwreathes the conscience of Nietzsche; an epergne that jives the ephemera of my soul, which durst the past to forget the pain of the present moment; a lazaretto that subsumes the lebensraums of God, whose eloquence is like a Mahayana for the devil's mesnes. It's a me-tooer's sanguinity, which redes its own credibility, like a Rousseauist idler; a post-apocalyptic possiq for left-behind Salomes in Antigua; a conclave for an underground Cytherea; a Nubian nudnik who capers his own delusions like a pagan; it profits not the soul to prog its own sigil and reeve its own satiety… yet it is oblique, like an obsequy about the future of poetry; a new age populist in a manta, whose vim cannot abstain its own lacuna, like a cosmic bridge to Xanadu… They ratiocinate my tempers, fling my soul upon upheaval sheets that demean my artistry, and then they expect apian parodies to be sensical to their nonsense---their semi-setose faces should be repudiated by this; they would weave my raiment several fold they are so thick with dispute. Are they steeplechasers of intellectualism? Am I the fetlock of their outrageous study? Or are they steeplejacks of attainment and I am the cloud they seek to wound? Tell me. Do I wear these brooches to 'scape my vanity? It's their peccancy to make themselves meditate after they interpret my pedestrian flight---they cannot pebble my pebbledash, nor may they assume that I am not their outlier's penologist. Ay, they ponce about, without proof of propaganda at their fear's disposal; they are propagators of razed war-time beaches that peel the temperance of every grain, which once they dampened with too true tears, but now do so as compassionless pioneers of Sodom, who forge their own distractions--- to be deontic toward God. But, this is the truth, Solomon: while I swim in the ataraxic pools of Sodom, they drown in their own pretensions. But you… your strokes of genius are different. Your mind is more prone to empathy. Compassion nurses you rotten like a nomad… The mind's a book uncommon with its words---be as niveous unto me as an untutored page, and I'll debunk your mannerisms like a lounge-lizard at Cleopatra's grave, who would neaten the Neanderthal's repose with the neoteric dreams of a no-hoper, since you know that Ambition is as hatred in love's mirror. The oleander's marvel is as the ordnance of a fly. The peddler's providence is as common as the politician's extro-version. The peroration of a dying man is not licensed to hold the mirror with so base a shelter. Must I perjure equality, and raven the feathers of a nightingale, to accost the introspect of my throat upon the depth of every groan, or hums too tangible to hurdle the vengeance of hysterics? Ha, ha! We are not abstained, nor shall we ever embrace a moggy; when the comedian cathects our delusions. O but does not gibberish sound sweet to he who's jealous of the crook who

now yelps his dissimilation to the canapés,
who try to pillory his gazes and reason with
his madness? Would you enlighten a shadow
to debunk it? To you my ethics are trite; how
revive something you are convinced cannot
find a breath if its lungs are more diseased
than the laugh of men who yet do not get the
joke? You think you can cozen my charades,
and in them find the offense of a nifty
fellow, though they are his defense; how
dare you be mirrors unto anyone but
yourselves. But the median is unbalanced,
and the preamble is caught within the crypt
of a fly on the wall; do not quarry the dust, if
it would dirty the paraffin's pledge to tidy
the smoke like a mirror. There's no beauty
to be had in a room that's filled with despair.
Indeed, the door to genius is opened by
madness, but madness alone shuts the door
to its own duplicity, like a windowless
apprehension of the senses… but what, alas,
would the epigraph on literature's tombstone
be?

"You will never be same…"